THE
LACE CURTAIN
MURDERS

THE
LACE CURTAIN
MURDERS

(A Romance)

SOPHIE BELFORT

New York

ATHENEUM

1986

The lines quoted on page 99 are from "The Pity of
Love" by W. B. Yeats. This poem appears in *The
Poems of W. B. Yeats*, edited by Richard J.
Finneran (New York: Macmillan, 1983).

The lines quoted on pages 41 and 42 are from poems
Numbers 303 and 664 by Emily Dickinson. These
poems appear in *The Complete Poems of Emily
Dickinson*, edited by Thomas H. Johnson (Boston:
Little, Brown, 1960).

Library of Congress Cataloging-in-Publication Data

Belfort, Sophie.
    The lace curtain murders.

    I. Title.
PR6052.E39L3   1986   823'.914   85-48128
ISBN 0-689-11801-5

FOR MY HUSBAND

"My beloved is mine and I am his."

"New England towns lead, in general, happy lives."

ALEXIS DE TOCQUEVILLE

THE
LACE CURTAIN
MURDERS

(I)

WITH SOLDIERLY CALM, Alec Maxwell, Her Britannic Majesty's consul general in Boston, pulled on a pair of heavy gloves and set to work. He removed a placard from the tangle of barbed wire strung between his brass door knocker and the ornamental ironwork fence that surrounded his ravaged rose garden; then he addressed himself to the wire itself.

"Alec, don't you think it should be photographed first?" his wife asked. The Maxwells had returned, minutes before, from a weekend in Maine to find their doorway barred and their garden devastated. Nell Maxwell thought that persons daft enough to wreak political vengeance on flowers ought to have their lunacy recorded.

"I should not like to appear in the *Globe* in my gardening gloves," he replied, "although that might recall

3

the more sympathetic Britain of potting sheds and victory gardens." His wife knelt on one knee, scrutinizing the green oaktag poster that he had laid on the top step: white letters, fastidiously stenciled, read BRITS OUT! THE RAPE OF IRELAND MUST STOP!

"Nell, it's nothing at all."

"It is Mary Agnes O'Pake again, of course. She filches art supplies from the high school. Molly Rafferty told me, and she's decided to stand for Congress."

"They don't stand here; they run. Is Molly old enough?"

"Quite old enough, but it's Mary Agnes who is running. And I do know the idiom, dear. I learned Urdu so as not to disgrace you elsewhere. The incumbent, that dear old Mr. O'Malley who looks so frail, is even more ill than he appears, Molly tells me; and he is not expected to run again. Mary Agnes O'Pake has not had the decency to delay her campaign until he announces that he is retiring. Scattergood College, where Molly teaches, is in the district, you know; and she says that a number of the young women are exercised over Mary Agnes's candidacy. They think the Right-to-Life movement is grooming her to challenge the senior senator."

The last loop of barbed wire dropped to the stone steps, coiling as it fell. "New wire, unused hitherto, it appears. This can't be from the high school. Come in, my dear, I don't think they'll have booby-trapped the front hall."

"They?"

"She."

"Acting alone?"

4

"Unaccompanied, certainly, by anyone more dangerous than herself. Are you tired, Nell?"

"No. A little," she admitted.

"Then tell me about Miss O'Pake's ambitions for higher office."

"Molly watches her, did you know that? I recall the first time we met Molly, one of her students had won a fellowship and she was here for the reception. That was right after Mary Agnes had paraded about the State House with seven or eight men purporting to be from the Provisional IRA. Molly had seen their ceremony on the Common, and she told me that Mary Agnes didn't even know the words to 'A Nation Once Again,' thick as she pretends to be with the Provos. That outraged Molly—she's so thorough herself."

"Yes, a wholly admirable young woman. But you were telling me about the election?"

"Oh, yes. Mary Agnes has announced; and all the usual men—lawyers, house agents, insurance salesmen—are lining up, rather more discreetly, to enter as soon as O'Malley withdraws."

"Let's hope one of them beats her. Thus far, Irish-Americans in responsible positions have been exemplary. No undertakers in the race yet?"

"Heavens, no; after all, the O'Pakes are embalmers themselves. Mary Agnes's father still practices, if that's what it's called. Do you know the American for that?"

"I do not."

"But the interesting thing from Molly's point of view, and rather difficult really, is that Elizabeth Brewster, the president of Scattergood, may run herself. She's getting

5

restless, Molly said, and keeps quoting Virginia Woolf about Tolstoy living in a suburb and not being able to write *War and Peace*, and George Eliot fighting in the Crimea and transcending *Middlemarch*. How could one do that, though, improve on *Middlemarch*?" Nell mused.

"That is precisely what I ask each time the passage is quoted to me, generally by ladies with ample leisure and privacy and several rooms of their own. But I should think many people at Scattergood would be delighted to send Mrs. Brewster to the Crimea."

"No doubt. That dreadful dean, Christopher Boggle, for one."

"You do look beat. Let me get you a drink."

"No, not *framboise*, Alec. Plain brandy. Thanks, dear." She took a few sips and then said quietly, "I worry about James."

Their eldest son had chosen, after going down from Oxford, to join the regiment in which his father and both his grandfathers had served; and he had been sent almost immediately to Ulster. Their younger boys—on Easter holiday, Wallace from Brasenose and Robert from Winchester—had been sailing with their parents that weekend, talking a great deal about James. Alec and Nell had convinced them to spend the remainder of their vacation in Maine, rather than popping in to surprise their brother in Londonderry.

"I worry too; but the danger in Ulster is so idiotically random. I honestly think that he's no more likely to be hurt in the line of duty there than in a car crash anywhere in the world. And now, my dear, if you'll excuse me, I want to see if any of our rosebushes can be salvaged."

"Of course. Give me a moment to change and I'll help you."

Molly Rafferty looked disconsolately out her office window at the miracle of landscape gardening that was Scattergood College.

What this place needs, she thought, is boys from Queens.

She taught the Renaissance and Reformation; many judged her a likely candidate for the long-vacant Hannah Wilkinson Scattergood Chair of the History of Human Betterment. Hannah's son, Nathaniel Scattergood, a Quaker toffee magnate, had supplied many of the requisite carbohydrates to the diet of nineteenth-century factory hands in the north of England and in America. He had left most of his millions to temperance (and God alone, Molly thought, knew whether Scattergood himself had believed that the fellowship of the pub fostered revolutionary upheaval, while sweets consumed at home contributed to social peace); but some of the profits had gone to endow Scattergood College, first a ladies' seminary, now a women's college.

The azaleas, one had to admit, were remarkable: orange and pink like Gauguin's early landscapes, almost but not quite savage, opting like Scattergood's alumnae for the banker instead of the painter, but only after a struggle. Molly sighed. Two years before, on an afternoon as perfect as this, Danny Bloom had walked into her office—she remembered precisely the way the bushes had looked, the colors that had massed and then resolved into individual flowers, she could still see each stamen and pistil, and then blurred again—and told her that he was going to marry a senior, his student, his graceful, rich, deferential student. Dan's fiancée was the daughter of a prominent man whose substantial fortune, based on the timely introduction of synthetic fibers into moderately priced women's wear, supported two major publications: the programmatic neoconservative organ *Civic Virtue* and the more literary and explicitly Jewish monthly *Continuity*. His future father-in-law, a Polish immigrant who had long been indifferent to his Jewish origins, was now zealously rectifying that omission. Molly had wished Dan happiness. She had heard the rumors. She had taught the girl herself and thought her rather incurious. That boded ill for Danny's happiness—or perhaps, on the whole, it did not.

Once, more than once, she had thought how funny it would be to be called Molly Bloom, to live with the predictable academic jokes, "Does she ever say 'no'?" She had said "no" while Danny was still married to his first wife, a handsome but apprehensively sullen young woman from Hunter College. Molly, who had been brought up to take special pains with people who looked ill at ease, had had several long conversations with Debbie Bloom before she became acquainted with Dan, though not before she had noticed him in class. She had noticed him straight away. Debbie was not happy in Cambridge. She wished if they had to be there that Dan were in law school, not graduate school; she knew, Molly sensed, that she was losing her husband, to no one in particular but to the ambience, the wider horizons. She would rather have kept him, but she was inclined to cut her losses.

It was not until Debbie had determined to do that—

had asked for a divorce and gone back to New York to get a master's in library science—that Molly would consent to accompany Dan on any occasion that she could not present to herself as strictly professional: coffee and lunch one had, as a matter of course, with married colleagues. But she had been passionately drawn to him. Even now, a few weeks ago, seeing him when she was not prepared to see him on the "MacNeil-Lehrer Report," she had shuddered with longing.

There was a faculty meeting in an hour. The president, Elizabeth Brewster, had asked her to drop by at 3:30 so that they might walk together across that emerald lawn, so shaded by elms and beeches that it never wholly dried. It was always morning on Scattergood's turf, always dewy. "My love . . . doth endure vicissitude and season, as the grass." Oh, why can't you forget him, Molly asked herself, exasperated by her own fidelity. She collected her papers, students' essays, her reading notes, a book—a small, suggestive Italian work—and locked the door behind her. Bess would want to know about Newnham. It appeared she really did plan to run for Congress. If she won, Molly thought, she could take her relevance with her where it belonged—into politics—and we could get on with education here.

Bess Brewster greeted her with a question. "You live in Newnham, I think, Molly?"

"Yes, I do. I like it a lot."

"What is it you like?" she persisted, as they crossed the lawn to the meeting.

"Its ethnicity." It's a nice change from Scattergood, Molly added silently.

The congressional district John James O'Malley had

long represented arched like a rainbow up and out of Newnham, where O'Malley lived, through blue-collar suburbs that resembled the more prosperous wards of the city itself. Triple-deckers, duplexes, and small split-levels were interspersed, occasionally, with Greek Revival and Victorian houses—towns where, as the Irish said, you could touch earth, and front gardens were filled with climbing roses, cosmos, gladioli, and tomatoes. At its base, its southern and western extremity, shaped like a pot of gold, lay the township of Trafalgar, enclosing most of Scattergood College. The town was three times as large in area as Newnham itself but settled in another pattern; and those differences, reinforced by snob zoning, kept voter registration within the district more than seventy percent Democrat.

Since the end of World War II, families had moved along that arc, and Molly thought Trafalgar aptly named: the town held as fast against truculent upstarts in its day as Nelson had against Bonaparte in his. Only the industrious and well-conducted, those who rose as ingratiatingly as Nathaniel Scattergood himself had risen, were welcome there. Now some of Trafalgar's children, the accomplished, carefully educated children of the suburbs, were hurrying back to the city. Molly had not grown up in Massachusetts; but her family had, elsewhere, got to their Trafalgar and a bit beyond. And she, hating it, had preferred Newnham to the rehabilitated sections of Cambridge and Boston favored by many graduate students.

Dan Bloom had teased her about her need for roots, in the old days when that notion had seemed comical to him, and had laughingly outlined a mini-series called

"Spuds." Molly had found his parody delectably funny, but would not move in with him in Cambridge. Her parents, she thought, would accept almost any marriage with their habitual high-minded good form; but shacking up would unduly tax their tolerance. And when Dan had ceased to urge her to live with him, she had bought a pleasant old house on one of Newnham's leafy streets.

(2)

Newnham and the neighboring town of Walden were represented in the Massachusetts State Senate by Mary Agnes O'Pake, the eldest of seven daughters of a prosperous undertaker. Six had been named after virgin martyrs, Mary Agnes herself, Barbara, Cecilia, Lucy, Philomena, and Agatha. The second eldest, Mary Magdalen, had done justice to her incautious name and married, when already in trouble, the feckless Patrick Moran, given birth to a boy and then to three daughters, the last born after Patrick had died of pneumonia contracted when he had fallen drunk and slept all night in snow so deep that it had forced the cancellation of his patron saint's parade. Mary Magdalen had supported herself after her husband's death, first as a waitress, later working in positions of increasing responsibility for a catering firm. She was also available to help with private parties, and her presentations were recognized by discerning partygoers. Whenever she could, she found occasional work for the youngest, mildly retarded sister, Agatha, who lived at home with their father and eldest sister.

Mary Agnes O'Pake, the firstborn and preeminent daughter, had deplored her sister's infatuation with a worthless man, her "weakness" in submitting to him, her marriage—even her tireless and uncomplaining efforts, after Patrick's death, to maintain her family unaided. It would have been far better if she had come back and kept house for them. Agatha did that ostensibly, but she did it very badly; and Mary Agnes did not dislike her widowed sister enough to deny herself the comforts of her efficiency. The woman's pride exasperated her; she should have been grateful they were willing to take her back. Mary Agnes had little, therefore, to do with her nephew and nieces until young Patrick was nineteen. Then, in an uncharacteristically generous gesture—for her solicitude for fetuses was matched by her disdain for bastards and for bastards manqués—she had taken her sister's boy with her for a week's vacation in New Hampshire. Young Patrick Moran, like his father and unlike most of the women in his family, had neither academic nor practical sense. There was no possibility of a career for him in politics or in the Church; his mother was preparing to swallow her pride and ask her sister to get him any job at all in the Registry of Motor Vehicles when Mary Agnes's hearty Irish friends, also staying at the cottage in New Hampshire, took the boy back to Belfast with them. Mrs. Moran, distraught and more angry with her sister than she had ever been, turned to her late husband's sister, the activist principal of Holy Sepulchre School. Sister Jude immediately telephoned some people with whom she had become acquainted over Vietnam and, more recently, Central America, and one senator, who recalled her vehemence with affection, returned her call. He said that he had no direct contacts with the people with whom the boy was probably staying, but that he would send someone to see her. A circumspect young man, not very optimistic, flew up from Washington shortly thereafter to confer with Sister Jude; closeted with her all a long, fierce March afternoon, he told her everything they knew and gave her some addresses. The addresses helped not at all. Sister Jude had nothing to report to Patrick's mother; and late that spring there was a scene between Mary Agnes and Mary Magdalen in which the sisters exchanged words like "slut" and "murderess."

Mary Agnes was not long troubled by her sister's accusations. Patrick had gone to end the many hundred years' enslavement of the Gaels—Mary Agnes was vague about precisely when it had begun. (Molly Rafferty had been tempted once, at a candidates' night, to ask her point-blank just who this Oliver Cromwell was and what he had done, but decided it would be a cheap shot.) If Patrick fell, many others, fine strong young men, had fallen before him; others must yet fall, countless others. Meanwhile there was the work at hand, constituent services which Mary Agnes performed conscientiously with the help of Michael Ryan, a self-effacing young man who had made himself invaluable to her father on the business side of the funeral trade. When, a few years before, Mr. O'Pake had concluded that Ryan did not have enough personality to succeed him, he had turned him over to Mary Agnes. She shared some of her father's sense about people's uses and the limits of their usefulness, and she soon found that for many but not all things she could rely on Michael Ryan absolutely.

They routinely worked together twelve hours a day, placing people in nursing homes and veterans' hospitals while demanding welfare cuts, finding unnecessary jobs for unqualified people while denouncing bureaucracy, preventing evictions while fighting rent control. Molly thought it would be hard to find in advanced capitalism—not that Newnham was very advanced; she would put it herself, not counting fast-food establishments, at about 1850—someone who embodied more contradictions than Mary Agnes. But especially Molly seethed over the reverence-for-life contradiction. How could anyone raise money for the IRA and support a Human Life Amendment?

The primary would be early in September. Bess planned to begin campaigning as soon as she finished with commencement, the reunions, and a college fundraising swing through the Sunbelt. She judged that Molly Rafferty might be very useful indeed—she lived in the largest blue-collar city in the district and seemed to know all about it—if she could be persuaded to stay. She would be, most regrettably, officially on leave at the end of the spring semester; and very eager to go, it was said, and do something about Jansenists in Tuscany. But Molly had disappointed Bess once before: Bess had much admired an article Molly had published earlier that year on Mary cults and had invited her to a lunch about women's studies. Bess was anticipating the lunch would be heavy weather, because the chairman of the Physics Department, Clara Meicklejohn, would be there; Miss Meicklejohn had been saying to everyone for months that she had taught science all her life to anyone who cared to learn it but that, as far as she could see, women's science, like black science before it, was an imbecility. Bess had hoped Molly Rafferty might counter Miss Meicklejohn's objections, but she had not been much help that afternoon. She had said that many issues in women's history were important. She herself was interested in the appropriation, so ubiquitous and so lamentable, of the Virgin by the not-to-put-too-fine-a-point-on-it forces of the Right, but none of that could be understood without broader knowledge of the political and social context. She thought that a "women's studies" major was not, on the whole, a good idea; liberal education should not deny differences between people, but above all it ought to emphasize common humanity. And, she had gone on to say, rather heatedly, that students should not be permitted to major in paranoia.

"Spoken from the heart, Ms. Rafferty," Dean Boggle had interjected, "or thereabouts."

Bess, seeking to salvage something, had asked if Molly would teach a seminar, when she returned, on medieval and Renaissance images of women. "Yes, I suppose I might," she had said, "but chiefly I am interested in heresy."

"And if I am not mistaken, Ms. Rafferty, also in pariah capitalism?" Christopher Boggle had asked with silken malice. And Molly had replied, "Absolutely. Where would Scattergood be without enterprising

Quakers and Unitarians, rich Dissenters like old Nathaniel himself?"

"And how inspiring," the dean had continued, "that for many ambitious young persons *virtue*, whether private or *civic*, is not its own only reward. It is one of the happy *continuities* between the nineteenth century and our own."

"Your own success exemplifies that, Dean," Molly said graciously.

Clara Meicklejohn told her many friends that Boggle's conduct in dredging up Bloom's nefarious jilting was the most disgraceful thing she had witnessed in thirty-five years at Scattergood College; but that Molly had been exceptionally game and the remarks had been passed off. To her good friend, the Hellenist Cornelia Newman, she said, "I could have murdered the dean. Molly was just beginning to get over it."

"The whole affair was heartbreaking," Mrs. Newman agreed. "You know how philo-Semitic those highbrow Irish girls invariably are."

"Cornelia, why does Boggle persecute that young woman? She has always been civil to him; but he took an immediate dislike to her."

"An immediate fancy, I suspect. Molly is as unlike Boggle's wife as anyone could be."

"Of course, Cornelia, I wonder I never saw it myself. Neither he nor his spouse has, so to speak, the lineaments of gratified desire."

Unlike Miss Meicklejohn, Bess Brewster had never troubled to get to the bottom of the exchange. The dean had seemed somehow to have offended Molly but, really, he was invaluable and a pillar of women's studies. He had been supportive from the start, abandoning his own work on the politics of James Fenimore Cooper—of course, that had depended on Native American funding and money did not come any softer—to devote himself to an issue central to women's studies at Scattergood: hysterical frigidity among Victorian ladies. He had especially impressed Bess Brewster with his sensitivity to the illuminating gynecological problems faced by William Graham Sumner's sisters, cousins, and aunts.

Bess mulled it over: if Molly did go abroad she could not give day-to-day advice about the campaign; on the other hand, once she was safely in Italy, discussions about the women's studies major would proceed without her pithily expressed objections. Mrs. Brewster decided not to interfere: there was something to be gained either way. That night she received the first threatening phone call; a thick and agitated voice, almost incoherent in its anger, blurted, "A woman's place is in the home." She ignored it. After the third, and much more coarsely phrased call, she mentioned them to campus security.

(3)

MARY AGNES O'PAKE received similar calls and asked for police protection. She was much aggrieved—a *mother's* place was surely at home—but she liked to think of herself as wedded indissolubly to the Cause. The governor agreed with her completely, she was as free from a woman's ordinary cares as, say, a nun; but because others might not grasp the distinction, he saw to it that she was escorted everywhere by a state trooper.

That officer waited for her now, ill at ease in the one leather armchair kept for students' fathers and visiting clergy in the antechamber of the principal's office at Holy Sepulchre. Holy Sepulchre was a convent school of the most refined sort, very different from the parish grammar school he had attended; but glimpses of nuns still unmanned him and made him again a slow, tremulous child who could recite neither the catechism nor the multiplication tables. All those never forgotten terrors—the hush and flurry of the sisters' habits, their apparition around corners so noiseless that boys doubted there were feet beneath their skirts—made him rotate his wide-brimmed hat ever more rapidly through his red fingers. He stretched out his thick legs, limbs that did not show to advantage in the jodhpurs and boots of the State Police, and then guiltily drew them back and sat erect again.

"No, I will not allow it. I cannot believe that you would suggest it. It is absolutely out of the question." The principal's voice carried through a solid and well-fitted door.

Terrible, Thomas Driscoll thought, terrible when the Church lets you down. She's getting nowhere with that nun.

Senator O'Pake challenged the principal indignantly. "Why don't you let the girls hear the truth about Ireland? What are you afraid of?"

"I have already told you that I welcome your participation in a discussion of Irish issues, but it must be a balanced discussion to which I will invite other speakers." Sister Jude spoke quietly, her hands clasped in her lap by an effort of will. In ordinary conversation, she often gestured; but whenever she felt tempted to hammer a point home with her fists she forced herself to sit decorously and speak softly. "What I positively refuse to permit is collecting money in school to support random violence."

Senator O'Pake, dressed for her next engagement, a colleague's retirement dinner, in ombré chiffon mounting from mint to Kelly green and white kid gloves, rose angrily. "You support revolution everywhere but in Ireland. You claim to want freedom for a lot of spicks but not for your own people. I won't give a dime to this school, I won't even come to the communion breakfasts, until it has a new principal." She slammed the door behind her as she left the office; but Driscoll was on his feet before the door closed. "I'm sorry, ma'am, Senator," he said, "I'm sorry. I heard what she said."

The senator was flushed with fury. Driscoll looked admiringly at her and said gently, "She doesn't understand what you're trying to do. Some people don't appreciate it; but a lot of us are grateful to you." Driscoll wore pinned to the collar of his leather jacket a shamrock crocheted by his mother; Mary Agnes O'Pake stepped to one side as he opened the outer door for her and nodded her thanks.

Sister Jude watched the senator's driver, standing outside the school's iron gates, help the pair into the backseat of a black Cadillac. Heaven knew she wanted Holy Sepulchre alumnae to be forceful women: many, even those of the senator's sheltered generation, had made contributions to the Church and the community. Some were spinsters, many more were married to men locally influential. Mary Agnes O'Pake was—apart from Lizzie Hennessy, who had gone to Radcliffe and married the stroke of Harvard's heavyweight crew and become, as Liz Putnam, national president of Planned Parenthood—its most famous alumna; but Sister Jude had always mistrusted her. She herself was interested in the doctrine of just war and despised rodomontade. She altogether welcomed the efforts of decent Irish-Americans to discourage contributions to the IRA; moreover, though she knew she ought to be more forgiving, she detested the O'Pakes. Her younger brother Patrick, an engaging boy whose prompt, ineffectual contrition for his many sins had wrung her heart until she had seen him anointed on his deathbed, had married Mary Magdalen O'Pake, been made miserable by her relations, and drunk himself into an early grave.

Nonetheless, the issue of Northern Ireland and of Irish-American support for the IRA must be faced, though not as the senator wished it to be put. Sister Jude decided to call the Archdiocesan Speakers' Bureau. Perhaps they had someone who would denounce terrorism explicitly. Explicitly. None of that unsatisfying mumble, that deploring of un-Christ-like actions wherever they may have occurred, of which she had so wearied. She wanted an unmistakable condemnation, one that used proper nouns. She made the call, then crossed herself and returned to the budget for the next academic year which lay before her on her desk.

Sister Jude had made Holy Sepulchre an excellent school, adding academic rigor to its longer-standing traditions of devotion and gentility; and she had fought, thus far successfully, to keep it a girls' school. There had been school closings and consolidations throughout the archdiocese, and the cardinal wanted Holy Sepulchre to admit boys. Sister Jude objected; not, she said, because she was opposed, in principle, to coeducation, but because her girls, coming from the sorts of families they did, hesitated to compete with boys. And she would not throw their minds away. Let them at least grow up learning the rudiments, sure of themselves. But, the cardinal remonstrated, girls fall in love. And what sort of young man will they find in the secular colleges her graduates increasingly attended? The scandalous example of Elizabeth Hennessy Putnam's involvement with Planned Parenthood made it abundantly plain, he believed, that his concern was well founded. And her career, although it was the most flagrant, was not, he suspected, unique. Would it not be far better for the girls of Holy Sepulchre to get to know good Catholic boys?

Would His Eminence, Sister Jude had replied, admit girls to a hitherto all-male Jesuit high school on the same grounds? No, it was not the same thing. Was it not? Why not? This inconsistency, and others like it that she observed in the Church, did not trouble her faith, which was unshakable, but they strengthened her resistance.

(4)

AT THE END OF MAY, Molly Rafferty turned in her grades and, as she did each spring, picked a bunch of pink lady slippers in the Scattergood forest. She was arranging them at home when the phone rang.

"Molly, it's Nell Maxwell. Are you done with the term? Won't you come for supper? Alec is in Washington."

Molly, who had not much wanted to spend the evening finishing a book she had agreed to review, a book that promised to surpass in fatuity anything its prominent author had previously written, accepted gratefully.

"I'd love to. When shall I come? Would you like some lady slippers?"

"Heavens, yes. I thought you couldn't pick them."

"They aren't public ones, they belong to the college.

I thought I was entitled to a few, and I picked them very carefully. They are bulbs, aren't they?"

"No, dear, orchids I think. Just a tick. I've got the field guide right here." There was a sound of tissue-thin pages being turned. "Oh, poor things," Mrs. Maxwell exclaimed, "it says they propagate with difficulty and have extremely complicated relations with their pollinators."

"A common problem," Molly said.

"Pity," Nell Maxwell replied. "Do bring me one, Molly. It will console me for our slaughtered rosebushes."

"Did you lose them all? You said you thought you had saved a few."

"No, none survived. Alec is just sick about it, much worse than the time we were sacked in Lahore. We even lost the little wild bushes from the Isle of Skye. So much for fellow feeling on the Celtic fringe."

"These people are not Celts," Molly said. "They are Vandals."

"How right you are. Come at seven, dear," Nell said and rang off.

Molly heard about the bombing on the six o'clock news, wondered whether Nell would still want her to come, then remembered she was alone, and went early.

"All the soldiers actually killed were in Jem's battalion," Nell said. They were seated in the Maxwells' bowerlike sitting room, on the floor above the rooms used in the consulate for entertaining. Nell sat very straight in a Nile green silk chair, surrounded by objects that spoke well of her. Rajput miniatures, showing Krishna disporting with gazelles and peacocks, hung be-

25

side European still lifes. There was a notable Dutch painting of wild strawberries scattered on a Delft plate and, better still, an anonymous English study of translucent gooseberries heaped in a black basalt Wedgwood bowl. Tonight Molly did not notice the art at all; her gaze kept returning to the many photographs of the Maxwell boys: sailing, rowing, climbing; Jem lifting a very young Robert onto a Shetland pony; James and Wallace reading in different branches of the same apple tree—Nell had once explained that James coached Wallace through his History A levels. Wallace couldn't make out whether the gentry were rising or falling.

"Won't you have something to eat, dear?" Nell asked.

"Perhaps later," Molly said, hoping that Nell herself could eventually be persuaded to have something but sensing the time was not yet right.

Nell continued. "I've seen the early films. They were on television. The units weren't identified, but I could tell from the insignia, of course. Three privates, a sergeant major, and a captain and some bodies, not in uniform, that they are unable to identify—that, I am very much afraid, they cannot yet even count—but if they've got the ranks right and if he wasn't in mufti, he's not dead. Alec is calling Londonderry from the embassy. He said he'd call immediately he heard anything."

Molly could think of nothing to say, but she wasn't called on to say anything. Nell could not stop. "We were so contemptuous of pacifism. You know that Saki story, 'The Toys of Peace,' where people try to stamp out war by giving their children little figures of the benefactors of humanity, Herbert Spencer or John Stuart Mill, instead of toy soldiers. Alec and I agreed that was ridiculous. And Jem loved Kipling so. We never *glorified* war, of course. Only savages do that—perhaps even they don't really. But I must have read him 'Red Dog'—you know, in *The Jungle Books*, when Mowgli rallies the wolves to fight the dog pack that's seeking *Lebensraum*—I must have read it to him a hundred times myself. And I don't know how often Alec did. When he was very small, Jem said that Mowgli was like Churchill—or that Churchill was like Mowgli. And then there was Saint-Exupéry, about how intellectuals shouldn't be like pots of jam, kept on the shelf to enjoy after the victory. I remember how struck Jem was with that. I think *Pilote de Guerre* was the first book he read by himself in French."

She spoke fluently for almost an hour. About her boys, Jem especially, about reading to children, about honesty and violence. Molly said not a word, recalling something else Kipling had written that struck her speechless with agony: "That hell of self-questioning reproach which is reserved for those who have lost a child."

Still the phone did not ring. "I am so glad you are here, Molly. I want to say something out loud that I shall not say to Alec, or to Jem. I am so frightened, so afraid, he will be maimed or blind or impotent; and we who are sound will have to urge him to live a life we would not choose to live ourselves."

At last the call came. "It's all right, Nell," Alec said. "There were two convoys. Jem was in the decoy that took the route everyone supposed more dangerous. The trip was so absolutely routine they had trouble finding him afterwards because he was off duty and had gone off into the country to sketch."

"Alec, is this the truth? You're not sparing me till we can talk face to face?"

"My love, you can talk to him yourself in the morning. He's not reachable now because he wanted to stay with one of his men, rather badly hurt, until the lad's parents arrive. And that is God's truth and I will be home by the last shuttle."

Molly wept when she heard and would not leave. "I want to stay here until Alec comes, if you'll let me."

"I hate the IRA, Molly."

"I hate them too. Perhaps I should help Mrs. Brewster. Having another woman in the primary might help—that is, it might hurt Mary Agnes's chances. And I know some people who might be able to convince O'Malley to hang in for another term. Do you want some tea? Shall I read to you?"

"Yes, dear, why don't you read Ecclesiastes?"

It was nearly one when Maxwell got back—haggard, but wild with joy he knew it would be indecent to express. "Thank you for staying with Nell," he said, as he saw Molly out. "She's so fond of you. We never had a daughter. Just her boys. You'll get home all right? Got your car? I'll just put you into it then." He walked down the street with her to her parking place. "We'll see you at the Athenaeum next Wednesday evening? Good night, my dear," he said and shut the car door.

He returned to his wife and, holding her tightly, said, "Jem is safe tonight, Nell; but everything tells us it is going to be a bad summer. I think the stiff upper lip will be called for time and time again."

(5)

THE NEXT MORNING Molly called Margaret Donahue, the president of the Newnham Teachers' Federation, a woman whose political judgment she had reason
to respect.

"O'Malley can't last another term, can he?"

"No, and he won't try. He knows he's dying and he
wants his successor chosen in a regular election. He's an
old-fashioned Democrat," Margaret said with asperity,
"remember them? He believes that special elections are
a hardship for people and that anything can happen if
turnout is low."

"It certainly can," Molly agreed. "How does it look
now for Mary Agnes?"

"Too good. Half the district owes something solid to
the O'Pakes."

"The president of Scattergood is thinking of jumping in."

"Sight unseen, I'd vote for her against our green Pasionaria."

"It would be a real help to Bess to talk with you," Molly said. "Can we set up a lunch?" She had decided that the race, though a small thing, was the sort of thing one had to get involved in. What was it French Socialists had said about the Dreyfus affair, not the battle we would have chosen but one we must fight?

Margaret Donahue welcomed a chance to fight Mary Agnes. She expected shortly to hear of a setback attributable in part to the senator's influence. Joe Calabrese, the city solicitor, had asked to see her at eleven. No doubt the mayor had finally decided not to call for a referendum to set aside the tax cap and had dispatched Joe, whom she liked very much, to her cluttered office in the high school to break the news to her. It did not sweeten her mood to learn her surmise had been correct.

Several suburban towns had recently voted to repeal the ceiling imposed on local property taxes. Margaret believed that unless the citizens of Newnham could be persuaded to do the same, the city would soon be unable, even minimally, to educate its children. But the mayor had talked it over at length with lots of people and everyone had said no way, not in Newnham. Newnham ain't Trafalgar. Joe said that he himself had argued for it longest and Margaret believed him; but, in the end, he too agreed that the vote would go better later. People were not hurting enough yet. If the summer was really hot and they closed one or two of the three pools and laid off more policemen and teachers, maybe then. It wasn't pretty, but there it was. Joe told Margaret that Mary Agnes, who had once represented Ward Eight on the City Council, had been especially vociferous. "Government has to learn to live within a budget, just like everybody else," Joe mimicked the senator's querulous voice. "The people just won't stand for it. And besides, if someone is really . . ."

"I can just hear her. Did she say 'truly needy'?"

"Of course not, she's not a Republican. She said 'if anyone really needs help they can come to me.'"

"We will see a reemergence of machine politics. There's nothing to stop it but the municipal unions, and they are run by morons, by and large. Has Mary Agnes learned to call all this 'reprivatization' yet?" she asked.

"No, but you read her statement on parochial schools supporting tuition tax credits?"

"I couldn't put it down."

"It covered everything; Mike Ryan must have written it," Joe said.

"We don't think we can fight that head-on in this city. We'll just talk about cost and leave the constitutional issues to those whose constituencies will understand them."

"Don't sell the city short, Margaret."

"That's what Molly Rafferty said. She thinks the grandchildren of Sacco and Vanzetti must be out there somewhere. She was asking if the Sons of Italy might have been a Red Shirt organization, a free-thinking alternative to the Knights of Columbus."

"Did she ask them? I'd like to have been there when she sailed in and asked them that."

"No, but she did look into it obliquely and found less

antagonism than she'd hoped. I told her there wasn't a lot of secular humanism around; but honestly I don't think that's the point. People here can't afford to be disinterested. And I know the people who are paying tuition think they are supporting two school systems. We're hoping we can beat this with the elderly who object to any new spending on the young. But, Joe, how much help will Mary Agnes actually get from the churches?"

"Some. I don't think Sister Jude will let the Holy Sepulchre Alumnae do anything for her; but it will be hard if she makes tuition aid her issue. And Sister Jude herself may want another Irishwoman in the House, added to those already inquiring about missing or murdered Maryknolls; that might offset her scruples about Mary Agnes's Irish policy. And Washington could tone that down; she might be made to put Ulster in perspective, you know, the Speaker and both senators all being Irish."

"Maybe, but Mary Agnes would fight that. She doesn't like to take advice from men."

"That's true," Joe said ruefully. He dealt with her often and found her more galling every time. "And if what she really wants is to run for the Senate eventually as an outsider—"

"Outsider," Margaret interrupted bitterly. "That's a good one. She is so goddamned lace curtain."

"Who's going to run against Ted Kennedy, Margaret? A welfare mother? Well, I've got to go. The mayor wanted me to let you know and to say he was sorry. He really is, and so am I."

"Thanks, Joe. Are you getting ready for your wedding? When is it, Saturday after next?" She looked at her calendar; like Mary Agnes, she went to wakes and weddings.

Joe grinned. "Yeah, I've been ready . . ."

She smiled back. She was old enough to enjoy passion vicariously and intelligent enough to know how much it mattered. Her young assistant Teresa Dellachiesa had moped around the art room all year because of unrequited love and now, because of the projected cuts in the school budget, faced unemployment as well. Margaret thought she ought to go and have a word with her.

Teresa sat at an easel, at work on an inept but yearning charcoal sketch of a man's head. She looked sad and scared. She had already been notified that her contract would terminate in June. No one would be left in the Art Department except the chairman, Miss Donahue. Tax cap legislation. No arts. No frills. Just the basics. Miss Donahue was a power in the teachers' union. She was tough; and although she had said she would do what she could for Teresa, she would be angry when she found out how many supplies were missing.

But Teresa was far more unhappy about something else. Her two best friends from high school were married already. Laura had a baby and Tara was expecting one; Teresa had seen her last week, fretfully but ripely pregnant. And she was going to be a bridesmaid again when Patty married Joe Calabrese. Nick would be at the wedding; he'd see how nice she looked in her pink gown. But she knew he did not want to marry her. He never tried anything; and his sister Laura said that sometimes that was a good sign. It had been, she confided, with her husband, Frank, before he proposed. But Teresa knew.

She knew that it didn't mean that Nick loved her or respected her or anything, just that he wasn't interested. She rose as Miss Donahue entered the room and hastily covered her drawing.

"Teresa, art supplies are very low."

"Yes, Miss Donahue."

"Can we make it through next year with what we have in stock?"

"I don't know. Miss Donahue, there isn't much oaktag."

"That doesn't matter. Have we got something, anything, that will take charcoal, and watercolor?"

"Yes. But the oaktag, you know, for posters and collages. Miss O'Pake came in and took it. She said it was for nonpartisan purposes."

"Yes, her latest march on the BOAC terminal. Damn that woman. Have you heard? She's endorsed tuition tax credits."

"What?"

"Tax credits. Subsidies for private and parochial schools. Teresa, don't you read the newsletter?"

"Yes, of course, Miss Donahue."

"Have you found anything yet for next September? Would you like to do art therapy? There's a grant proposal in for that."

"I like to work with people."

"Yes, and you are very patient. I'll look into it for you. Now, Teresa, if Miss O'Pake comes in again, I want you to tell her that she can't use school materials. It was a trifling matter once, but we cannot afford it now. It's just unconscionable that she should care so little for public education and come in and rip us off. Do you understand? You can remind her that, as a state senator, she has an allowance for office supplies—and she can write them off."

"Yes, Miss Donahue."

(6)

Bᴇss Bʀᴇᴡsᴛᴇʀ read over her remarks on "Women in the Age of Reform." As president of Scattergood College, she had been asked to open, jointly with the head of Saint Maud's, oldest of the Oxford women's colleges, a major exhibition at the Boston Athenaeum. An exchange of letters had been found between Elizabeth Gaskell, the novelist and biographer of Charlotte Brontë, and Rebecca Cavendish, a Massachusetts woman of similar sensibility, herself the wife of a Unitarian clergyman who had lived in Lowell. Bess was looking forward to the evening's festivities; they offered an opportunity to meet people who might prove useful to her in many ways.

The letters Mrs. Gaskell and Mrs. Cavendish had so faithfully exchanged discussed the lives of the millworkers and their heartening efforts at self-improvement; the plight of the Irish in Manchester and in the New World; their daughters' lessons and how best to balance enthusiasm and discipline; and, with evident concern, the persistent error of Trinitarianism. Mrs. Cavendish reported that the notion seemed to have been strengthened in New England by certain advanced supporters of the rights of women who identified the Holy Spirit with the Eternal Feminine. "Why," she lamented, "when we have so laboriously freed ourselves from anthropomorphism, must these fools espouse *femino-morphism? Gyno-morphism?*" Molly Rafferty, who had xeroxed the choicest letters for her busy president, had written "DEAD RIGHT!" in the margin next to that. And Molly had made a précis of the rest of the correspondence and supplied historical background for the president's talk. She was happy to do it, she said; the letters were wonderfully combative. And besides, Bess had been raising money from Scattergood College clubs in the Sunbelt up until the very morning of the opening; Molly wanted to do all she could for someone who coaxed that much money out of Houston and Phoenix. But Bess intended to avoid theology altogether and remain on the uncontroversial ground of social service.

Bess nodded to herself as she turned to the last page of her talk. It was the paragraph already known among some of her faculty as the "half empty/half full" gambit: much accomplished, much remained to accomplish. How best ultimately to eradicate sexism? Perhaps she should call for a larger representation of women in public office. And that would not be entirely self-serving, Bess thought, for Mary Agnes O'Pake would be there too. Senator O'Pake had contrived to be invited under the misapprehension that the Warden of Saint Maud's was royalty. Disabused of that hope by a *Globe* staffer who told the story widely and malevolently, she gathered that the Irish were somehow involved—the reporter had grossly misrepresented the plot of Mrs. Gaskell's novel *North and South*—and determined to go anyway. She arrived exultant, for she had just heard that an ecumenical bookstore in Belfast had been devastated by plastic explosives; although there had been no loss of life, it was not expected to reopen.

The two candidates met for the first time on the marble steps of the Athenaeum's foyer. Bess had not heard of the bombing and could not account for Senator O'Pake's mood; after shaking hands, they went in together, followed by Miss O'Pake's state trooper. Officer Driscoll excused himself, made a quick tour of the building, and looked for the bar. The drinks looked good, but he was on duty and thought he'd better not indulge. "Thank God," he said afterwards, confiding to a fellow officer that as the evening proceeded he was "sweating jellybeans."

Bess Brewster was pleased by the austere grandeur of the building's interior, though she conscientiously noted there were no women among the busts that peered down into the reading room from pedestals that reached almost to the gallery railing. Surely, surely, she could persuade them to enshrine Julia Ward Howe and Louisa May Alcott in two of those spots. This was Boston, after all! And Emily Dickinson too, of course, though Bess could never understand the fuss made over her work. Molly Rafferty soon joined her and agreed that the Athenaeum was wonderful; no public buildings pleased Molly more than temples of learning, august and elevating. She listened to Bess's effusive thanks for her help with the speech and then went to look for Nell Maxwell, who was briefing the Warden of Saint Maud's on local dignitaries expected to attend. The Warden had been Nell's tutor at Saint Maud's and they remained close friends. Nell Maxwell had exerted herself to make the exhibition a success; she had unearthed, during the past year, in public and private libraries from Worcester to Leeds and in the Scattergood College Women's History archives most of the photographs, etchings, and memorabilia displayed with the manuscript letters; she had also arranged the catering for the buffet supper.

The talks were well received and, after some preliminary congratulations, people began to circulate among the glass cases. Bess Brewster saw Henry Hughes Putnam and his wife, Liz, accompanied by Mr. Putnam's vigorous mother, and hurried over to introduce herself to all three. The elder lady was saying to her son, "You see, Hal, in that photograph, there between William Ellery Channing and Mrs. Cavendish, it's your father's great-aunt Abigail Putnam. So like Liz in temperament, it's uncanny." Bess had what she judged to be a very satisfactory conversation with them. It was a shame, she thought, that a limit had been put on individual campaign contributions; abuses had undoubtedly occurred, but it did make it difficult for unknowns. Bess had remarked on that to her husband, and he had said, "Perhaps you are a *political* unknown at the moment, dear, but people will soon see your merit."

After Bess moved on to some media people, the Putnams were approached by an unannounced candidate,

Jerry Harrigan, the young mayor of one of the penulti-mate towns, one very near Trafalgar. Liz Putnam's back stiffened and she moved closer to her husband. Hal Put-nam greeted him cordially. Harrigan said he had come to assure them privately that although he could not say so in public, he was pro-choice and would, if elected, vote for, or at any rate not vote against, Medicaid abor-tions. Liz rallied to her national responsibilities as presi-dent of Planned Parenthood: she quite understood his position, she said; she welcomed such assurances from a man who had accomplished so much, from whom so much more was expected. But it was obvious that she did not like him. It was obvious, in fact, that if he touched her she would scream.

And so, Molly thought, would I. Harrigan was a boy-ish cutthroat, the sort of swaggering lecher certain Irish families brought up their daughters to shun. He reminded her of a young man who once called for her on a blind date when she was seventeen and he a junior majoring in strategic studies at Pius IX University in Washington. Her mother had taken one look at him and suggested they all play bridge. Her father had sat him down with a stiff Scotch; and they had played cards and listened to his admiring tales of Pio Nono's struggles with the Eu-ropean Left until it grew too late to do anything else. Kevin No-No had been a family joke for years.

Harrigan followed Bess Brewster's path from the Put-nams to the press, said a few words to an attractive tele-vision anchorwoman, and was soon deep in conversation with a Smith graduate who wrote editorials for the *Chris-tian Science Monitor*.

Molly found Nell and told her how much she liked

the exhibition. But Nell, hovering over the buffet table, seemed strangely flighty. She acknowledged that she found it difficult, after Jem's close call, to be in the same building, let alone the same room, with Mary Agnes O'Pake. "But look, Molly, how very lovely the *crudités* look. I must thank Mrs. Moran. She outdid herself for me again."

"Would you like me to keep an eye on things here for a minute?" Molly asked.

"No, dear, I'll find her later. But would you mind chatting up the French consul? He thinks we should have made an effort to include something about the French textile cities."

Molly did as she was asked and then, tired suddenly of the pious charities of Roubaix, slipped off into a reading room. She often worked at the Athenaeum, finding its amateur scholars pleasantly different from many academics she knew, who published indiscriminately, whether or not they had anything to say. She discovered one of the library's purest habitués, Ned Perkins, a gentleman farmer from Vermont, at work on his life of Emily Dickinson.

"Mr. Perkins, there's a party. Everything's delicious. You must go and have something."

"Oh, thank you, I will go presently. How are you? Is your work going well?"

"Well enough, but it was yours I was just thinking of. A line from Emily Dickinson sprang into my head not half an hour ago."

"She is so often apposite, isn't she? Which line was it?"

" 'Of all the souls that stand create / I have elected One . . .' It was rather fanciful. I'm supposed to be reviewing a book about marriage and the Reformation. It's a dreadful book, but I'd been thinking about choices in love and other sorts of election."

"She was a very Protestant spirit, quite peremptory. You know, of course, 'The Soul selects her own Society'? 'I've known her—from an ample nation / Choose One— / Then—close the Valves of her attention— / Like Stone.' But what precisely made you think of it? I'm always curious to know what summons up a particular line of verse."

"A woman who seemed very happily married. There was something so deliberate about her, a look of thorough and considered confidence in the man and the life she had chosen." Liz Putnam had, while talking with Harrigan, slid her hand through her husband's arm, as if to emphasize her stance. And Molly had seen the identical gesture before. Her friend Miranda Sternberg had done it at a party when a sloshed Yankee began decrying how ruthless, how really driven and brash, law students had become; and Sam Sternberg had replied, evenly, that hard times made everyone anxious.

"You speak of this wistfully, my dear, if you'll forgive me?" Mr. Perkins said, with more than customary gentleness. "But tell me, what is this party I've forgotten?"

"It's the opening of the Elizabeth Gaskell–Rebecca Cavendish exhibition."

"Oh, good Lord! Of course, your Mrs. Brewster and the Warden of Saint Maud's, extraordinary woman. I knew her at Oxford. And I suppose the British consul and his wife. Was it Mrs. Maxwell who struck you as so emphatically content?"

"No, it was someone else, though she is certainly another."

"Maxwell's a lucky man. I must go and see them." He hesitated. "Won't you go in with me?"

"No, I've been at the party. I think I'll go into the stacks and read for a while. You don't mind?" Molly felt a pang. Was he actually reluctant to go in alone? He was reserved, not reclusive—entirely at ease, surely, in such circles as would eddy about the Athenaeum. If he and the Warden were old friends, they'd have much to talk about. No, he had sensed her own forlorn mood. "You're very sweet to want to cheer me up," she said, "but I'm perfectly all right. Call me when you are next in Boston and let me make dinner for you. I'm working on something very nice with salmon and fennel."

"Thank you, I'll be sure to do that," he said.

Molly left him to collect his papers. The circular steps that led to the stacks off the gallery were dark; she felt for the switches, illuminated the stairway, and proceeded up. She thought she heard a rustle far back among the shadowy rows of bookshelves; but when she paused to listen, she could hear only the faint convivial noises that sedate parties produce. She went halfway around the gallery to the poetry section and turned on the lamp in a small bay of bookshelves. She thought she would read for half an hour and then go down in time to say good night to the Maxwells.

She took a volume of Catullus from the shelf. Generally the Latin she read was late and ugly, records of inquisitorial trials. It would be a joy to read something good, honest, and erotic. "*Basia mille, deinde centum, dein mille altera, dein secunda centum . . .*" "A thou-

43

sand kisses, then a hundred more, then another thousand . . ." She skipped restlessly on until she came to Ariadne, abandoned by Theseus, rushing wildly, incredulously into the surf after his departing ship: *"Perfide . . . perfide . . . Theseu.* If you were afraid to marry me, couldn't you have kept me somehow, carried me home with you as your slave? No hope; all is changed . . . *nulla spes, omnia muta, omnia sunt deserta."* There was as much fury in Catullus as there was honey. She read absorbedly until she was distracted by voices in the reading room below, hushed but argumentative voices, women's voices, one alternately peevish and authoritative, the other plaintive, frightened. She couldn't imagine who it could be. Neither of the voices was, precisely, educated, but there was some asymmetry in the conversation; perhaps a supervisor speaking with one of the serving women. Once again Molly heard, and this time she was certain she heard it, a rustle, a feminine noise, something like a skirt, but no footstep. Almost immediately there followed two shrieks, an appalling crash, then hysterical keening—a voice full of horror, lightened, perhaps, by a consciousness of having itself escaped.

Molly hurried through the stacks in search of the rustling sound, lost track of the light switches, and came out a full four minutes later on the opposite side of the gallery. People were rushing into the reading room now; all the lights were on. Mary Agnes O'Pake knelt over the body of a woman; Miss O'Pake's trooper bent over her, pleading with her to come away, to come with him into another, safer room. He shouted, to the world at large, for reinforcements. Alec Maxwell telephoned for a doctor and for the police. A bust, falling from its pedestal beneath the gallery railing, had killed one of the waitresses, Agatha O'Pake, the sister of the state senator and of Mrs. Moran, who had planned the menu and supervised the service.

It was, Molly thought, looking sickly down, very close to "her own mother wouldn't have known her." And those were precisely the words chosen by Officer Driscoll as he wiped his red and throbbing forehead to describe the scene to the detective who arrived presently: "Jesus, Mary, and Joseph, her own mother wouldn't know her; but she did look like her sister, you can see that."

"Yes, I can."

"I dunno what the governor's gonna say. Thank God it didn't hit *her*. Thank God. Can I take her home now? Please, Lieutenant, let me get her out of here."

"I think it would be better if no one left the building," the detective lieutenant said. "You may take Senator O'Pake and Mrs. Moran to a private room and lock yourselves in. But I will want to see them tonight."

"Jesus," he said imploringly, "she was their sister."

"I know that." Why, he wondered, do they always say that? Don't they know what percentage of American homicides take place within nuclear families? Not, certainly, among Irishwomen of the sort involved here, but better that no one leave.

Molly, too, thought that Agatha and Mary Agnes looked a lot alike. They were both birdlike, pinched, and very fair. Strawberry-haired girls they must have been, with translucent skin and pale blue eyes; both now bleached their hair, but the senator went to a better hairdresser. The dead woman's hair was a cheaper, more metallic yellow; she probably bleached it herself at home. That hair that didn't look like hair, especially in the brilliant light cast by the naked bulbs in the Athenaeum's unadorned ceiling lamps, was, apart from the blood, the most lurid note. She had been very decently dressed; her black nylon uniform with detachable starched collar and cuffs looked embarrassingly like her sister's lace-trimmed navy blue silk.

It had crossed the mind of several women present at the Athenaeum that Senator O'Pake did look like a parlor maid, and an extremely febrile and repressed one at that. Bess Brewster was the only one who gave tongue to the thought, late that night, to her husband, a kindly pediatrician who dearly loved her.

"I am not in the least worried about Senator O'Pake," she continued. "She appears to know nothing and nobody."

"Over the years, she must have made some friends here and there," her husband cautioned.

"No one of the slightest importance, it would seem. I had a very nice chat with the Putnams, most encouraging. And you'll never guess who else was there."

"Who?"

"Ned Perkins."

"We haven't seen him in years. How is he?"

"Unchanged to all appearances, spare, a little grayer, but still so very, very unworldly. He hadn't even realized the opening was tonight. I don't think the event was publicized in advance sufficiently."

"The Athenaeum staff may lack your flair for public relations, Bess. But Perkins seemed well?"

"Perfectly well, amiable old bachelor."

"He was always amiable. I think it's sad he never married."

"Does he like women?"

"He liked several while we were at Yale. Did he seem shaken by the accident?"

"He seemed thoughtful, but he always seems thoughtful. He was one of the first people questioned because he must have just left the reading room when the O'Pake sisters entered it. But he left the Athenaeum as soon as the detective was finished with him. He got a call that one of his cows was calving and rushed back to Vermont."

The police had been prompt. A squadron of state troopers had arrived almost immediately, for the Athenaeum was only a few hundred yards from the State House; and they were soon joined by a homicide contingent from the Boston Police Department.

Molly came down from the gallery and was sitting with the Maxwells and the Warden, Mrs. Brewster was talking to the press about violence against women, when the detective entered the large reception room in which the guests had assembled. Everyone, the very room itself, Molly thought, brightened noticeably. And it was not just the prospect of finishing up something disagreeable and going home.

Nell Maxwell put a name to it quickly enough. "What an extraordinarily beautiful man! Everything about him suggests the most radiant moments of the early Renaissance. What do you think, Molly? Pollaiuolo? Nothing later?"

"He moves, as you say, exuberantly," Molly said, "but

47

his face is thoughtful. I'd say Titian, maybe Pontormo."

The detective, whose provenance had been so quickly settled, approached them at last. "I am Lieutenant Hannibal from the Boston Police Department. I have been talking with some of the other guests. I understand that you are the lady who was in the gallery?"

"Yes, I am; and I was in the stacks, before I heard the crash."

"Could I get a statement from you now? It would be a great help." He looked at the Maxwells, as if they might be her parents; but Molly rose immediately.

"Yes, certainly," she said.

He led her into the curator's office, which had been put at his disposal.

"Your name? Yes. Address?" She gave it, and he looked at her closely.

"I've lived in Newnham for years, since I started graduate school," she explained.

"I live there too. I grew up there. What do you do?"

Isn't that interesting, Molly thought, do they ask women that now, before they ask whether they're married? Or perhaps he had noticed she wasn't wearing any rings.

"I teach history at Scattergood College."

"Is that why you were in the stacks? Were you looking up something?" The question was asked not quite deadpan, and their eyes met.

"It's just a nice library."

"Yes, it looks great," he said. "Now tell me what you remember."

"Starting when?"

"When you left the French consul and went into the reading room, prior to ascending to the stacks."

She told him everything she remembered, as carefully as she could, hesitating once or twice. "It did seem, though I couldn't conscientiously . . ."

"I don't mind if it's impressionistic. You seem to have been very observant."

She went on, trying to be thorough, trying to be precise, and found she could not take her eyes off his face.

At length he said, "Thank you very much. Would you give me your telephone number, in case I have any further questions? It's very late. Did you come with Mr. and Mrs. Maxwell? Are they waiting for you?"

"No, I came by myself," she said.

"I'll send someone with you."

"It isn't necessary, really." Did he suspect her? Was he protecting his witness? Was he merely chivalrous?

"I'd prefer it," he said, communicating both authority and solicitude.

"Very well, then, thank you. You will call me if I can help you?"

"I will."

The patrolman who escorted Molly to her door checked in with the detective forty minutes later.

"Did Miss Rafferty recall anything else on the way home?" Hannibal asked.

"No, she didn't, but she asked how long you had been a cop," he joked.

"Is that what *she* said?"

"No, Nick, those weren't her very words."

"Try to remember, will you?" he said, sounding as if he wanted to know.

49

"I do remember. She said, 'How long has Lieutenant Hannibal been with the force, or is "with the force" something they only say in books?' "

"And you said? I can guess . . ."

"Yeah, I did, I said it: 'The force is with him.' "

"And what did she reply?"

"She said, 'I bet it is.' She smiled when she said it."

"Thank you." That answer had been very satisfactory, and Hannibal returned to the work at hand. "Her story's very clear. I had her retell it a number of times, all consistent but none of them pat. Of course she's a professor, she must be used to repeating things."

"No kidding. She told me she was a teacher. She lives in Newnham."

"Yes, I wonder if Joe Calabrese knows her. It's too late to call him. She'll be a very credible witness eventually. Is Driscoll back yet?"

"No, sir. Nick, the governor gave him instructions, personally, not to leave Miss O'Pake. He's going to sleep in the funeral parlor tonight."

"Let's go see him. We're just about finished here. Tell them they can remove the body. This case won't turn on any of the coroner's subtler points; but I think the building had better be sealed until we can go over it again in the morning."

Lieutenant Hannibal learned little when he questioned Driscoll, except that Mr. O'Pake, however grief-stricken by the loss of Agatha, positively refused to let any man but himself sleep under the same roof as his remaining maiden daughter. Driscoll could be accommodated in the adjoining mortuary; but O'Pake had made sure he would be comfortable there before retiring to say his nightly rosary. Driscoll mentioned as Hannibal was leaving that Mrs. Moran had not stayed to help her sister break the news to their father, but asked to be taken home, so that she could tell her daughters of their aunt's death before they heard it on the news.

The technical people adamantly ruled out accident. The bust (it had been of Wendell Phillips) that had fallen on Agatha O'Pake had shattered but it was already being reconstructed. There did seem to be scratches, caused by some metallic object, around Phillips' ears. It must have been pried off its pedestal, grasped perhaps by some forcepslike object; it could not exactly have been aimed, just tilted or prodded until it fell. Those scratches and the evidence, for which Hannibal had some independent confirmation, that someone besides Molly Rafferty had been in the gallery made it seem indubitably murder.

So Hannibal began the next morning tediously checking the guest list, catering staff, employees of the Athenaeum—and inquiring into the pathetically small circle of Agatha's friends and the much larger and more disputatious circle of her relations. But even among these last, he found unanimity on one point. No one could have wished to kill Agatha. Senator O'Pake must have been the intended victim.

Several individuals willingly confided their suspicions and none of these theories, remarkable equally for squalor and vagueness, could be dismissed. From several people he heard of the firing of Billy Foley, one of the senator's drivers. Some said he had been suspected of stealing petty cash, others that he made unauthorized use of the cars. It was suggested, also, that he had been too attentive to one of Mary Agnes's nieces, Kitty Moran. Some managed to fuse these elements into a more sustained and damaging narrative. A few thought he had been canned for refusing to kowtow to the senator. No one knew if he had found another job.

If not the hapless Billy Foley, then who? A crazed patriarchalist out to get women in public life? Bess Brewster had told him about the menacing calls she continued to receive. She thought the person sounded desperate, suffering perhaps from some hormonal imbalance. Could the blow have been meant for her? It was unlikely anyone could mistake the president of Scattergood, massive and hearty, for that little waitress.

Perhaps it had to do with the well-established IRA connection? Dissident factions therein? Paisleyite hit squads operating in America? That was more than implausible, it was incredible. Besides, there had been no phone call claiming responsibility; and on every side of that conflict there were people who called up to take credit every time a truck backfired.

Closer to home, Lieutenant Hannibal looked into loansharking, construction fraud, building code violations, protection broadly construed. He made careful inquiries among the big- and small-time players of hardball in the city. Everywhere the same note was struck: they would not touch Mary Agnes O'Pake. She did not make trouble for them, they would not make trouble for her. She was better than a lot of other politicians, they told him, better than a lot of politicians who might get elected if Newnham's neighborhoods continued to change. They were, Hannibal reflected, men who saw the coming of young professionals as the worst of several calamities that could ruin a neighborhood.

Political opponents of Senator O'Pake? Possibly. She had an interest in several nursing homes and saw to it that all their patients received absentee ballots and all the help they needed in marking them. It was likely, too, that a certain number of proxies were cast on behalf of deceased former patients. There might be fiddling with Medicare and Social Security checks, as well as with absentee ballots; but nothing that raised the stakes to murder. She didn't need to be that crooked. Her victory margins had been solid for years, and her family was rich by Newnham standards. Her aide Michael Ryan spoke at length with Hannibal, candidly and sensibly, the detective thought. Nothing seemed in the least unusual about the campaign.

There was a famous feud between Mary Agnes and Margaret Donahue dating back to the fourth grade at Queen of Heaven; hard feelings over a spelling bee, which the Donahues charged the nuns had thrown to Mary Agnes, led to Margaret's expulsion and grew into a lifelong commitment to public education. But Margaret Donahue had been speaking in Worcester, at a rally for the First Amendment, in constant sight of one hundred and fifty people all day and much of the evening in question. And when Hannibal duly questioned her, she struck him as someone whose rage over tuition vouchers would stop short of homicide.

The senator's personal life, like that of her dead sister, appeared to be absolutely chaste. She was nearly fifty years old. It seemed unlikely that someone had seduced or been seduced by her years before and could bear it, the guilt or the shame, no longer. She was, in the State House, very much one of the boys, asexual, in a sense—men would not use their crudest language in front of her, but functionally, she was more crony than broad. Yet someone had most certainly tried to kill her and had killed her sister by mistake, either because they looked very much alike, the more so by the coincidence of their dress that night, or because one could not calculate very nicely where Wendell Phillips would fall to earth.

The character of Molly Rafferty, who had looked to him like a woman who meant what she said, was vouched for by Joe Calabrese. Joe had first met her in connection with Property Owners for Rent Control. She lived alone in her house in Newnham; sometimes students stayed with her; invariably when she traveled, someone, visiting academics or students, lived in the house. He and his fiancée had had dinner with her a few times. His mother liked her very much. Patty liked her too. She was a nice person. Molly wasn't a suspect, was she?

No, Hannibal didn't think so.

"Interested for some other reason? She's coming to the wedding. Saint Sebastian's at two o'clock Saturday."

"I know, I'll be there."

(7)

SAINT SEBASTIAN'S was a new church, almost suburban in its charmlessness. Molly was appalled by the
iconographic poverty of its windows; the 1960s hadn't
been a good decade for stained glass. She had arrived
promptly and watched as others were seated. There he
was, the detective, Hannibal. Nell had been exceedingly
merry on *that* subject. "Hannibal, Molly, just fancy!
And he is, too, so commanding . . ." She had been almost skittishly gay. Molly had attributed it to her relief
over Jem.

She had thought about Hannibal too, from time to
time, more than she acknowledged, and certainly more
than had been good for the review she was to have finished for Friday. He was with an older woman, his

mother. Yes, it must be. He nodded at her and she returned his greeting. Yes, he was unsettling.

Molly hadn't been to a Catholic wedding since her youngest aunt had married, but that was before Vatican II had made itself felt and she was curious. Why wasn't there a book in a rack on the back of the pew? It would be interesting to see how the liturgy had changed. She would hear it, of course; but it would be better to read it first. And she would have liked something to do other than watch the affectionate banter between Lieutenant Hannibal and the lady who was doubtless his mother. He looked a little older than Joe. How old? Thirty-five? Thirty-three? There was no mistaking what they were talking about: Why hadn't he? When would he? What was he waiting for?

Why indeed? Molly thought. Unsentimental, probably, and nobody's fool, but not a misogynist. No, disdain for a large and undifferentiated category of human creatures wasn't in him. Perhaps he hadn't found the right woman? When you get that unoriginal, she told herself, you work on something else; and she redirected her attention to the windows.

Soon the murmuring stopped and the music began, Joe's mother was seated, then Patty's, the procession began, and Molly felt cold, very cold. Father Reynard was to marry them; Molly liked him. He was a taut, lucid Québecois with the all-seeing smile one saw on busts of Voltaire. She had met him in Rent Control, too.

Molly had been to lots of weddings. She and Danny had gone to a few together, and although she was averse to ritual, she was always caught up in the solemnity of it. Love really had to do with Life and Death. These people would conceive children together and watch over them with the unutterable love and dread that Nell and Alec felt for Jem. And finally one of them would die, and the other would wonder if he'd loved enough. Father Reynard caught her eye and smiled, reminding her that it was a celebration; and she wondered, as she smiled back at him, how much he knew about each of the people there that day.

Molly got slightly lost on her way to the reception and arrived after the party had begun. She preferred that to being early as she had been at the church; though characterless churches were by no means alien to her, she felt alone and hostile in them. But here, in this ongoing, already constituted gaiety, she felt perfectly at home. At some point they would dance the tarantella. She must tell Bess, when she started campaigning in earnest, to remember that if she didn't know the steps, which she certainly wouldn't, to clap in time with the music; that's what Molly always did.

Hannibal was dancing with one of the bridesmaids. He danced well and seemed to be talking earnestly with the girl. And why not? She was beautiful. She was ravishing. The deep rose color of her dress suited her perfectly. He walked her back to the head table and Molly noticed that, as they talked, he cast the briefest glance at the band to see if they were about to resume playing or about to break.

Just then, Mrs. Calabrese came over and hugged her. How nice of her to come. Was she having a good time? Did she know anyone? Molly had just said she wouldn't have missed Joe and Patricia's wedding for the world when Hannibal's head and shoulders materialized over Mrs. Calabrese.

"Molly, this is Nick Hannibal," Mrs. Calabrese said, "an old friend of Joe's. They went to Boston College High together. Nick, do you know Molly Rafferty?"

"We met a few days ago."

"Yes," Molly acknowledged, "at the Athenaeum."

"Oh, were you there too? It must have been hard for you, Molly, and living all alone . . . to think of something like that."

"Lieutenant Hannibal was very kind, Mrs. Calabrese. He had someone take me home afterwards."

"Nick, why don't you dance with Molly?"

"I was just about to ask her." What else could he have said? But he said it with an alacrity that did not altogether surprise her. Father Reynard had once remarked after a decisive meeting in which their views had prevailed, "Miracles aren't unexpected. That's a misconception. If we weren't preparing for them, we wouldn't recognize them when they come."

Molly had been waiting for Nick Hannibal. He guided her to the dance floor, taking her elbow in a way once called "masterful." Not, Molly thought briefly, masterlike, that *would* be oppressive; more like full of mastery—perhaps a syllable had dropped out. As soon as he had space to turn and face her he took her in his arms.

It was, she thought afterwards, the way it was supposed to be. Or rather, the way it was no longer supposed that it should be or had ever really been. A mystification. He held her closely as they danced, not too closely—he wasn't a boy; he must have lots of opportunity to hold women—but there was a throng dancing now and he held her closer. It was a long medley. The torso and thighs on which Nell had so unhesitatingly pronounced felt the way they were supposed to feel, the visual sensations transformed into tactile ones.

"Your address surprised me. Are you gentrifying us?"

"I'm not gentry."

"You're not simple."

"Neither are you."

They danced in silence; they both noticed that Margaret Donahue, always alert, was attempting with little success to engage the abandoned bridesmaid in conversation. Molly tried to place the girl. Teresa Dellachiesa, quiet girl, taught—what was it—art. The music ended and Nick released her hand, but he kept his arm around her. Molly leaned, imperceptibly she thought, against him. He spoke quietly close to her ear. "That bridesmaid, sitting with Margaret Donahue, is a friend of my younger sister. I'm going to dance with her now, until they serve the first course. I'll call you tomorrow, may I?"

He seemed reluctant to go.

"Yes," Molly said, slowly and distinctly, terrified that she might not be making herself understood. "Please do call me tomorrow."

"Good, then, I'll call you tomorrow morning."

"Yes, please."

"I have your number."

"And I'm in the book."

"Good. Good night."

"Good night."

Molly sat down and watched as Teresa surrendered herself to him with a readiness as painful to see as it was easy for her to understand.

"How's everything? You look cataleptic." Margaret Donahue had moved on to her. "Am I interrupting a reverie?"

"No," Molly said decidedly. Reverie was not the word.

"I heard you were there."

"Yes, I all but saw it happen."

"And you think?"

"I think someone must have meant to kill Mary Agnes. The papers say that the victim led a heartbreakingly inoffensive life. And she did look, even lying dead, quite a lot like Mary Agnes."

"They questioned me, did you hear? Had I murdered for the public schools? Would I shed blood for the vision of Horace Mann? Frankly, I hope I would if it ever came to that, though it never occurred to me to personalize the problem in that way. But Mary Agnes is a poisonous bitch, much meaner than you'd think. I know that the most-often used political adjective of our recent past, near future too, I am afraid, 'mean-spirited,' might have been coined to describe her; but it goes beyond that."

"Really? I thought politicians like Mary Agnes were usually very loyal and generous, in their own circle at any rate."

"Many are. She's not. She is hateful. But I never thought to harm her. Besides—" Margaret paused and said superbly, as one speaks lines one has never expected to utter, "I have an alibi."

"Yes, you were in Worcester, the night of the opening. I was torn myself because school prayer seems so pernicious to me; but a close friend was very involved with the exhibition."

"Is that where you met Nick?"

"Nick Hannibal?"

"The one you were dancing with, the one who all but carried you back to this table five minutes ago, surely you recall."

"Lord, Margaret, I hope you go about the union's business with more tact." Women who affected frankness to that extent put her off. Nell did it too, but with tearing high spirits that softened the effect. "Yes, I was exhaustively questioned by him, the night of the everyone-seems-to-think, I'm sure he thought, murder. Do you know him?"

"I know him some. He went to BC High and the University of Chicago."

"That's an interesting sequence," Molly said.

"Yes, and then into the army, Europe not Asia. When he got out everyone expected him to go on in classics, but instead he joined the police. When he had just begun, was still riding a patrol car, there was a melee at the high school. He helped break it up, and, in the tussling, a little *Aeneid* fell out of his pocket. I remember I helped him pick it up afterwards; some pages were loose in Book IV. He seemed abashed, the way kids are when the particular page falls out of that year's dirty book."

"Really." Book IV? Wasn't that the desperate love of Queen Dido? "I can't imagine him abashed. He's, um, charming."

"That he is. The Dellachiesa girl pines for him, but I don't think there is anything between them. I wish I could find a job for her next year. My staff is being cut. Do you know of anything?"

"I might. Which staff? The art department or the Teachers' Federation?"

"Which do you think? Does that girl look as if she has a scrap of militancy in her? Better for her, in more than one area of her life, I imagine, if she had," Margaret said.

"Lots of Scattergood faculty send their children to suburban public schools and those, as I am sure you know, still have art departments. I'll ask. You're very good to concern yourself with people's problems."

"I'm a switchboard. It's part of my job."

"Thank you, Margaret."

"Thank *you*."

Molly left early; she went home and looked it up and thought Virgil had put it very well. She had not remembered, or perhaps she had not understood when she first read it, quite how accurate the poet was. He understood the hallucinatory yearning that made you hear and see the man after he had gone. He knew about the debilitating fire, *mollis flamma*, that burned through your body, *et tacitum vivit sub pectore vulnus*, through the aching hollowness.

Teresa stayed at the wedding reception and caught the bouquet, but Margaret could see she did not put much stock in it.

Molly woke bolt awake at six o'clock Sunday morning. She tried to go back to sleep, decided that was hopeless, and reached for a book. At ten o'clock Nick called and asked her to have dinner with him that evening. They fixed a time. He hung up and she remembered that the chairman and his wife were having the department for drinks. She called them. Miriam answered and Molly excused herself, something had come up.

"Bring him," Miriam said, matter-of-factly.

"I can't. No really, it isn't. Thanks anyway."

He took her to an excellent small restaurant on Newnham's not yet fashionable waterfront. The proprietor, Sal Valenti, came over himself to take their order, and Nick introduced him to Molly. She listened with attention as he described his specialties and readily agreed when he concluded by suggesting that she let Nick order for her.

"You've won him completely," Nick said when he had left them. "Is there anything you'd like that I didn't think of?"

"Nothing," she answered, startled by the certainty she felt that he would have little trouble anticipating any of her wants.

He helped her to some antipasto and asked her what she had taught the previous semester. They had, they found, much to say to each other. It was not the sort of first date that reminded Molly of Ph.D. orals: a series of tedious, predictable questions, lines of conversation carried doggedly to the bitter end out of a sense of responsibility or malice, gambits abruptly dropped when some suspicion was confirmed. Plainly, they liked what they saw in each other. Sal came by their table from time to time, more than hospitable, encouraging; Molly asked Nick if they shouldn't ask him to join them for coffee. "Yes, certainly, nice of you to think of it," he said.

Sal brought another chair and a bottle of indescribable liqueur, searingly potent, with a strange, fugitive aftertaste. "I've never had this before," Molly said, "it's like an herbal anisette. What's it called?"

"You like it?" Sal was beaming. "It's a family recipe. I make it myself. I think it was my great-, my great-great-grandfather, who, uh, adapted it."

"Adapted it? From what?"

"From, excuse me, are you a devout Catholic?" Sal seemed uncertain how to proceed. It did not occur to him, Molly thought, that she might not be a Catholic at all, but she had left the Church, in her own mind, definitively.

"No," she said. "I'm not."

"The recipe has been in my family for more than a century. My ancestor was a peasant boy, but very clever. His mother wanted him to be a priest, but she was too poor to prepare him for the seminary, so she had to settle for making him a monk."

Molly nodded sympathetically. Nick smiled at her absorption. He had heard Sal tell this story before but never to so rapt a listener. She had said she was interested in church history; he trusted Sal to suppress the bawdier elements of the tale in the presence of a young woman so unmistakably a lady.

"The monastery he entered made a famous, a very secret *liquore*. When he was a novice, they sent him to gather herbs for the brew. At first they did not even tell him which ones they actually used, just to gather everything from a certain hillside. Later, as they trusted him more, they told him which ones to pick, but still he could tell there was some secret ingredient. Now," Sal paused, "this was a time of great troubles, of, how do you say, *insorgenza* . . ."

"Insurgency, yes," Molly said. "Which one?"

"Ah, Nick used to ask me that too." Sal seemed pleased that the pair had that in common. "But I don't know and he couldn't figure it out either."

Nick explained, "I think it was probably the French in the 1790s; but it could have been later. It might have been one of the many failed insurrections of the nineteenth century. The political details have been lost." Other details had, of course, been lovingly preserved: the deflowering on the abbess's bed, for example, and the sudden necessity to hide underneath it when that august lady entered her chamber with a stable boy; the complications following the arrival, soon thereafter, of her confessor. Molly did have that air of immaculate refinement Nick associated with girls from select Catholic schools. On the other hand, she was warm and good-humored; and there had been nothing repressed about the body he had danced with the previous evening. "Tell Molly the rest of the story, Sal," he said.

Sal needed no encouragement to continue. "It was a revolutionary time, a bad time for the Church and for the nobles who protected it. The brothers decided that they must make an enormous amount of their drink and seal it in a cave, in case the monastery was looted. But one herb was missing, the one they had not yet told my great-grandfather about. Now, they said, he would have to get it himself, alone. And they told him where to find it. Can you guess where it grew?"

"I can't imagine," Molly said, although, familiar as she was with the folklore of Catholic countries, she was fairly certain where it must have been.

"Go ahead," Sal urged. "Take a guess."

She appealed mutely to Nick, whose eyes revealed nothing save that he was enjoying the moment hugely.

"I can't guess," she said, "please tell me."

"It grew," he said, "it grew in the walled garden of a convent."

"No," she exclaimed.

"Yes," he insisted.

"How extraordinary, a convent garden."

"Walled," Nick said.

"Yes," Sal continued, "walled and tended by a young nun of angelic beauty and purity. Well, it was, as I told you, a revolutionary time. There are many stories about their, uh, courtship, but such stories it is best for lovers to tell each other when they are old and remembering their youth. Both of them left their orders, my ancestor joined the rebels, taking his bride with him into the hills. And I am proud to say," he concluded solemnly, "that no man in my family has been celibate since then."

"That is a wonderful story," Molly said.

"You liked it?" Sal asked. "And you like the drink?"

"Very much, but I like the story even more."

"But the drink is very good, too," Nick said.

"Yes," Sal agreed. "It is excellent. You understand. We do not sell it. We do not steal from the Church. But we make it for our families and for our friends and for their families when they have them."

Molly fully realized how ridiculous it was to blush at this simple statement of policy, but she could do nothing to prevent it. "That's very generous of you," she said.

"It's a beautiful night," Sal said, getting up and standing behind Molly's chair. "Why don't you go for a walk on the docks?"

"Would you like to?" Nick asked.

"Yes," she said. "I would. Thank you so much for dinner, Sal. Everything was memorable."

"I'll see you again," he said contentedly as he walked them to the door, "soon."

"Sal is very direct," Nick said when they were outside.

"He's very nice," Molly said. "And the soul of delicacy in his story-telling. You must know some things he left out."

"I'll tell you another time," Nick said. "I want to look at you in the moonlight for a while. You have a sort of delicacy too, the air of a girl from a Sacred Heart school."

"Nope," Molly said, "I do not. My parents sent me to public school."

"Then your mother did," he persisted.

"Yes, you're right. Mother hated hers and swore she would never send her own daughter to one like it. It's odd you should be so certain." It was curious he saw that in her. Danny had told her, in the first sweet intimate weeks of their affair, that he had been afraid to ask her out; she reminded him of the girls, utterly off limits in his boyhood, from a school his friends called "Our Lady beyond the Pale." And they had made love and laughed about her unapproachability.

"This topic makes you sad," Nick said. "I'm sorry. Let's walk to the end of the pier and look for jellyfish in the water."

The water was black as onyx and floating, pulsing through it were the transparent bodies of hundreds of moon-jellies, trembling parasol-shaped membranes, shapes only faintly visible, but luminous.

"It's a miracle anything can live in this harbor," Nick said. "Particularly something so fragile-looking."

"They seem to be thriving," Molly said. "There's a whole colony, or school or whatever. They probably don't need to eat many of the other things that can't survive in this water."

"Can you sit down on the end of the pier? The dress you're wearing looks somewhat fragile itself," he said. Her skirt shimmered around her legs in a way not unlike the undulations of the moon-jellies. He put his coat on the rough planks of the dock and they sat, side by side, in silence for a while. His presence dispelled, more readily than anything else ever had, her recollections of Danny Bloom. Nick was watching her face in the moonlight; she was pale, wore no makeup, her lips just a shade darker than her face. She thought that he would kiss her, but he did not. After they had sat in silence a while longer, she said that Hannibal had always been a favorite of hers and that the notion in Robert Frost's poem "Hannibal" about the "generous tears of youth," shed for lost causes, captured something she loved about teaching history—but that was so deplorably unprofessional she had never admitted it to another academic.

"Our name is anglicized, of course."

"Yes, I thought so. There was a Cardinal Annibale."

"No relation. My father saw the Church about the way Hannibal's father saw Rome. He didn't positively swear me to vengeance, but I was taught to mistrust its politics."

"I've often wondered how much Italian anticlericalism made it to the New World," Molly said.

"A considerable amount," he said, "as you saw to-night. Sal and my father were good friends."

"Hamilcar," Molly pursued a line of thought, "Hanni-bal's father, must have been something for his son to live up to. But, in another way, he's not terrifying at all," she said eagerly. "He's reassuring. Do you know the legend that he refuses to sacrifice Hannibal when he's a small boy and the elders of Carthage are called upon to offer up their firstborn? Hamilcar won't do it, unlike Abra-ham with Isaac."

"Or Brutus," Nick continued, "who ordered the exe-cution of his own sons when they threatened the Repub-lic. *Fiat justitia, ruat coelum.* Or Agamemnon. Daughters are sacrificed too, remember. And you know what hap-pened to Carthage. The great civilizations like Israel or Greece or republican Rome faced the truth about the conflict of love and duty. And they or their principles endured."

"That's quite right," she said, "but I've always felt sorry for Clytemnestra. Even before her husband sacri-ficed their daughter to get his war off on the right foot-ing with the gods, it can never have been much fun to be the sister of Helen of Troy."

He looked at her curiously and she said, "My sister is a knockout." But that sounded so much like fishing she added quickly, "But notwithstanding your father's atti-tude toward Rome, didn't Mrs. Calabrese say that you went to BC with Joe?"

"Yes, I did go to high school there. My father had died by then; and my mother—perhaps you know the pattern—was more devout, though she's by no means

69

fanatical, and she thought a Jesuit institution would be a good place for a fatherless boy. I wasn't fatherless, though. The memory of him was so strong."

Nick picked up a handful of pebbles and sand from the dock and tossed it out over the water. They scattered the moon's reflection, driving fragments of light off in all directions to illuminate the oily iridescent surface of the water. "Moonlight and motor boat fuel," Nick said.

"And how was BC?" Molly asked. "What was it like?"

"Good school," he said. "I did Latin and Greek. And the Church . . . it really isn't monolithic."

"If I had a dime for every time in the past five years that I have said that some institution or movement wasn't monolithic—medieval Christendom, Bonapartists, Marxists, the Democratic Party. I did the introductory course for a while." She gestured impatiently, dismissing the lot of them, zealots and trimmers.

He caught her hand and held it, drawing her nearer to him. "Well," he said, "there's the Marines. They're monolithic. I preferred the army."

"And the police?"

"Yes, maintaining any order at all, seeking any justice, seems an unending struggle. Those dualist heresies that interest you so much have a certain plausibility. Good and evil are evenly matched."

"Detectives and historians know that!"

"And it seemed to me merely honest to acknowledge, you know, the line of Kipling that Orwell liked, 'the uniform that guards you while you sleep.'"

"Yes," she said, "or to wear it. I understand perfectly. The son of a friend of mine said exactly that."

"Son of a friend? He must be a precocious kid."

"Oh, my friend isn't my contemporary. He's a grown son. He's in a"—for some reason, Molly did not say: "Guards regiment"—"in the army himself."

"Really? Which branch?" He seemed, she thought, most interested.

"I'm not sure. I've never met him, only heard about him."

"It's late," he said rising, "and you are cold." He put his coat and his arm around her shoulders. "Are you free Tuesday night? I'm going to be tied up tomorrow checking on the people who were at the Athenaeum before the accident, presumed crime, and not seen thereafter."

Molly recalled that she had not seen Harrigan or the anchorwoman or the Smithie from the *Monitor* while everyone was waiting to be questioned.

"Yes, let me make dinner for you. I can cook. I like to cook. My house? At seven?"

"Fine. I'll try to be prompt, but things sometimes come up."

(8)

MOLLY SPENT most of Monday at Scattergood: an hour closeted with Bess Brewster, talking about primary voter turnout; an hour trying to pacify the indignant parents of a Texas debutante who wanted to take a year off and work on a kibbutz; not enough time working on her review; quite a lot of time looking at Renaissance drawings left to the college by a wealthy former student who had not managed to graduate with the class of '24 but who held no grudges. She drove home giving, she recognized, more thought than was warranted to the question of dinner. *Vitello tonnato?* Was that like serving somebody corned beef and cabbage? But what was better in the summer when someone had an erratic schedule and might not be able to get away?

Tuesday she was in an awful state and spent the afternoon at the Athenaeum with Nell, hearing about how she had found all the photographs to illustrate Mrs. Gaskell's and Mrs. Cavendish's various points.

"And did that lovely *quattrocento* detective need to question you again, dear?"

"The face is later. It's more complex. No, he did not question me. I saw him at a wedding though, and I'm having dinner with him tonight."

"How nice."

"And Sunday."

"Next?"

"No, last."

"Then he must have a sound mind as well. And I'll grant you the face."

"Nell, I can't talk about him—not that I can think of much else."

"Well, of course not, dear. This nasty candor about men is nothing more than a reversion to the gossip of the village well. Or the riverbank. Women bashing their laundry about on stones and bragging about their husbands' prowess or lamenting their shortcomings. I do try to learn the language wherever we go—and let me tell you, American feminists have much to learn in expressing disappointment. Frightful! No loyalty, no delicacy. You would not believe the metaphors for impotence in the East. Naturally you cannot talk about him if you care for him."

And she changed the subject abruptly. "I wish more people could see exhibitions like this; I was talking with Mr. McGonnigal, the Irish consul, about something. We were thinking it might be constructive to have some sort of Anglo-Irish festival, emphasizing common culture.

Swift and Burke and Shaw and Yeats. There's so much, it does seem a shame."

"You could call it 'divided by the same language.' "

"You think it wouldn't do any good?" Nell asked, disappointed.

"You and Alec weren't in Boston when the Museum of Fine Arts did the Celtic Gold show—in the same spirit of community outreach?"

"No, dear, we weren't, how did it go?"

"I was at the opening with the cousin of a friend of mine, Winthrop Boyden, who's very public-spirited. It was what you might expect, a lot of Brahmins with green carnations in their buttonholes." Winthrop, Miranda Sternberg's cousin, Molly recalled, had looked the most incongruous of them all. "And there was someone from the archdiocese looking embarrassed."

"Why was he looking embarrassed?"

"Because the pagan artifacts were beautiful, barbaric, gorgeous, they just knocked you out; but the crosses and reliquaries, all the Christian things, seemed tinny and derivative, utterly without conviction. It looked as if it had been downhill all the way after the Druids."

"How sad. Oh, it's nearly five, and you're having dinner with that glorious young man. You must run along."

Nick called at 6:30 to say he would be late. He was sorry. Hoped she hadn't made anything that wouldn't keep. She said she would be glad to see him whenever he could get there. He came at ten and ate appreciatively, but he seemed preoccupied and roused himself to thank her formally.

"I hoped you would like it. What kept you?" Molly asked. "Is it something you can tell me about?"

"I don't see why not, now that I've finally straightened it out. One of the unannounced candidates was on the list I told you about."

"Yes, Harrigan," she said.

"Do you know him?"

"No, but I recognized him and I did think he had left before you began questioning people."

"He wasn't there afterwards and neither was the television personality with whom he's said to keep company. Mary Agnes is expected to bring that up as soon as she finds it necessary. He lied about his whereabouts. The woman from Channel Nine said he'd been with her for more of the night than he had been. And his wife said he had been home all night, even during the time we know he was at the Athenaeum. There were so many discrepancies that I thought I was on to something. But as I pursued it, it became apparent that the anchorwoman did not in the least want to protect him, much less precipitate a divorce and marry him. She thinks that sleeping with men like Harrigan is one of the perks of her job and that the exposure might enable her to go national. His wife doesn't care how many women he sleeps with so long as he does it discreetly; because she's eager to get to the top and she certainly can't get there on her own."

"Was Mrs. Harrigan that frank?"

"No, but she is that transparent. And Harrigan himself gives manifestly not a damn for either woman. He is a little worried about losing his children and very much more afraid of losing elections. But he didn't try to murder Mary Agnes to silence her because several people saw him at the Channel Nine studio within five minutes of the time the crime was committed. Do you find me reactionary?"

"Not in the least. I should think your evening's work must make you long for an honest crime of passion."

"Those shouldn't be romanticized. But the Harrigans are depressing. I couldn't wait to get here. You're so wholesome."

Sophia Loren I am not, she thought.

"Can you play *bocce*?" he asked as they lingered at the door.

"It's like *boules*, isn't it? I've played that in France."

"Tomorrow, or Thursday? I'm not sure which night I can get away."

"Either night would be lovely," she assured him.

"You are lovely, Molly. Thank you for waiting up for me tonight and bearing with my mood."

Molly turned on the radio after he'd left and heard—it was early morning Greenwich time—that two shopgirls had been killed in a suburb of Belfast opening up a cheesemonger's that had chosen, injudiciously, to advertise William of Orange Gouda. She wished someone had killed Mary Agnes.

Nick was well-known and eagerly greeted at Corvelli's and Molly was reasonably good at the game, to the openly expressed amusement of the patrons. She watched as the balls rocketed around and off the sides of the court and clustered into patterns around the *pallino*, the central target ball.

"I wonder when I see all those organized spheres if Galileo played *bocce*."

"Interesting question. Playful, provocative article there. You're refreshingly unprejudiced, Molly, for an Irish girl from the outer suburbs."

"I am *very* prejudiced. I have my own carefully selected ones."

"Am I heir to all the ages?"

"I think you know you've got more than the ages going for you."

They looked candidly at each other and, as if something had been agreed between them, began to talk of other things. Nick asked about the work she would be doing in Italy.

"I'll be trying to clarify the social context in which certain heresies took hold. It is curious," she said. "No one seems to know quite why a critical mass of weavers in a town for forty years generally produces a vernacular Bible and a denial of transubstantiation. And it's the continuity of the dissidence that seems so miraculous to me. The material conditions, what Marxists call the mode of production, the level of well-being, the international contacts, any of that can change or all of it; but once begun, there remains a kind of fidelity to dissent."

"I have an old Bible in Italian."

"I'd like to see it. Just the New Testament or both?"

"Both," he said. "The New Testament is incomplete by itself, too otherworldly. No sense of civic virtue."

"What?" Molly said.

"The Gospels, they lack *virtù*. Don't you agree?"

"Entirely," she said.

77

"Molly, you've gone very white. Is it too stuffy for you in here? Shall we go outside?"

"No, I'm fine," she said.

"Are you sure you're all right?"

"Yes, perfectly all right. Let's stay. I'd like to."

"Okay then. Come, it's our turn to use the court again."

"Speaking of weavers," he said when they relinquished the court, "let me show you something." He took an envelope from his inside breast pocket and shook a scrap of material from it. "This is a mixture of silk and wool. Is that common?"

"Not common, but very beautiful."

"Available here?"

"Yes, readily available as fabric. Harder to find ready-made. There was an Irish designer who used to use it a lot. Made rather covered-up and tailored dresses. That mixture makes up beautifully—dressmaking details are very pronounced . . ."

"You warm to the subject."

"My grandmother was a seamstress."

"We found this at the Athenaeum, caught in a sort of roughness, a headless nail, I think, on the gallery railing."

Molly knew the dress, she knew the shape of its collar and its mother-of-pearl buttons . . . but Nell had worked there diligently for weeks, several days each week.

"Yes," she said, "it's lovely cloth and it's just the sort of thing many women members would wear. This is expensive, but lasts forever."

"Yes."

"Why do you associate it with . . . with the tragedy?"

"We found it right above Wendell Phillips."

"Nick, do you want to know if I have a dress like this?"

"No, I think you haven't, though the colors would be becoming. You're clear, Molly. I've had policewomen try to get from where you are known to have been to where you would have had to be, and it can't be done in time, even in daylight. And those reenactments, I want you to know, were staged on Thursday morning, right after the crime. I would hate you to think I was . . ."

"Insincere?"

"Yes. I'm not. Look. Help me out. I don't know much about women's clothing. I'm not married. Don't laugh at me. I'm not a libertine."

"Neither insincere, nor libertine, and unmarried. That's heartening."

"I'm glad you think so."

"Do you have any evidence apart from these threads?"

"The physical evidence hasn't been helpful so far. I'm trying to play out some psychological hunches." He explained that fellow legislators regarded Senator O'Pake as an almost sexless being.

"That might provoke her to do something that had funny consequences," Molly said.

"Too much collegiality, you think, drove her at some point right around the bend?"

"It happens. That," she added, coloring, "is not an autobiographical reflection."

"How could it be?"

(9)

ON THE AFTERNOON before her aunt Agatha's funeral, Anne Moran, Patrick's posthumous daughter, stopped Sister Jude in the hall between trigonometry and French and asked if she could see her after school.

"Certainly, Anne. You have chemistry this afternoon, don't you? Shall I drop by the lab or do you want to talk in my office?"

"I'll come see you. I want to talk to you alone."

"What is it, dear?" Sister Jude asked as Anne sat down on the straight-backed chair in front of her desk.

"I'm worried about Mother, Aunt Brig." She called her aunt "Sister Jude" in class, but when they were alone she addressed her differently. She was her aunt's favorite, and she understood and treasured the favor shown her.

"She hasn't heard from Patrick, has she?"

"No, but I think it's been conveyed to her, she won't tell us anything, that someone may be bringing his effects."

"God help us all. His *effects!*"

"I overheard something. I thought that's what was said. 'Effects' is such a pitiful word. I hate to think of having effects like that."

"*Respice finem,* of course, dear, but don't dwell on it. I believe your life will have many other, many very good effects."

"I hope so."

"I am sure of it." Sister Jude had high hopes for Anne. She who was so undeceived by the world allowed herself wonderful visions: a medical missionary, another Nobel Prize, or perhaps research would be better still. Anne would find some hormone, some enzyme, that regulated fertility, something occurring in Nature, something more natural even than the Pill, something that anyone would have to admit was licit. Anyone. The most backward-looking, most obdurate, from the most besieged and be-nighted corner of Christendom. She checked herself; she could not permit herself that characterization of the pope.

But he had begun to fulfill all the misgivings she had felt at his elevation. In fairness, one had to admit, he was uncompromising about the responsibilities of the rich. But he had no experience whatsoever of free societies. All adversaries were not the Anti-Christ. Planned Parenthood was not the Red Army. She sighed deeply. But Anne would do something splendid, something that was catholic in the best sense of the word.

And Anne did mean to do good, though she was a

less exalted person than her aunt and had already begun to broach issues of group practice and flextime, in a general way, with an equally levelheaded and considerate boy from Portsmouth Priory whom she had met at a debate tournament.

"Do you have any idea when she expects to receive— what is it to be—a package? a courier?"

"No, I haven't."

"I can't do anything tonight; I have a parents' meeting. But I will go home with you after the funeral. And, Anne, you will learn this as a physician: it's often best to know the worst and face it."

That evening Mrs. Moran spoke briefly with a young man who came to her door but would not come in. She took the package he gave her into her bedroom, where she spent an hour alone with its contents. Then she called her daughters and asked them to pray with her for their brother's soul.

On the next morning, Friday morning more than a week after her death, Agatha O'Pake was buried from Saint Sebastian's. Agatha's wake, begun only when the coroner released her body, had been long and doleful, as befitted her family's position; and the funeral was the largest assemblage ever gathered about her. The press were mostly State House reporters eager to confirm the rumors that Senator O'Pake was the intended victim. There was chatter, of a not very reverent kind, in the church, until Father Reynard silenced it with his funeral mien, that calming air of decent resignation that Molly, when she first saw it, had called philosophical. The requiem mass ended, he followed the casket down the center aisle and stood at the door, dispensing terse but heartfelt consolation. Then scandal erupted: scandal, he instantly recognized, in its precise theological sense. Were the television crews there? He hoped not. It happened as the pallbearers lifted Agatha's coffin into the O'Pakes' best hearse.

"You, you should be in that box, you murdering bitch." It was Mary Magdalen Moran, whose horrified daughters, pale and red-eyed, were trying to quiet her. She was shouting at her sister, who clung to their father.

"You, you have never loved anybody. You claim to love Pop, but you have never, never cared for any living creature, no man, no woman, no child. You, you with your"—there followed a spate of obscenities so staggering that the one reporter who heard them all regretfully decided nothing could be done with them. "But not you," she concluded, "all you can do is kill." Father Reynard handed the censer to his acolyte and rushed forward; Sister Jude reached her first, slapped her quickly, and whisked some smelling salts under her nose. "I always carry them," she said when she and the priest discussed the scene later. "Girls still faint in church, in hot weather." She told her nieces to go along to the cemetery with their grandfather; she would take care of their mother. Father Reynard, seeing she had the woman in hand, went forward to comfort Senator O'Pake and her father; when he reached them he looked back to Sister Jude and she, who read his lips, inclined her head. She knew so many priests; he was one of the few whose blessing she valued.

Most of the crowd had heard only shouting, but enough people had heard enough to make up the rest. The story had spread through the entire city by noon.

"I simply can't believe it," Molly said to Nick. He had dropped in to ask her if she was busy Saturday. "You live so conveniently close," he said, "and I'd rather see you than just call."

"Margaret Donahue called *me*: she was at the funeral because the oldest Moran girl is practice-teaching and has gotten very involved with the union. The sisters have never gotten on, apparently, but Mrs. Moran, Margaret says, was always the sanest of the O'Pakes. Cheerful, resolute, competent; she brought up four children alone; the boy, I think she said, was wild, but the girls are exemplary achievers. Not just Monica, whom Margaret likes so much, but the others: the middle one, Kitty, does something like ice-skate or dive, where you have to be disciplined and get up early to use the pool or the rink or whatever; and the youngest, Anne, who's still in high school at Holy Sepulchre, wants to be a doctor."

"Did Margaret tell you all this this afternoon?"

"No, she just confirmed what someone else had already told me about Mrs. Moran. Mrs. Moran helps my friend Nell Maxwell with parties, and Nell says she's unflappable—and very frank and sensible. When Mary Agnes found out her sister was working for the Maxwells at the consulate, she really lit into Mrs. Moran."

"For collaborating by making watercress sandwiches?"

"Something like that. Mrs. Moran said she thought that people shouldn't live in the past."

"Not a sentiment you'd approve?" Nick asked.

"Ulster gives me pause. I'm not usually for forgetting, but that seems so hopeless."

"It's interesting that she sees the struggle in that light. When was this?"

"When Mrs. Moran started working for the Maxwells? Last fall I think, some time ago. Why do you ask?"

"Because I'm surprised to hear Mrs. Moran is working at the British consulate. Her son is more than wild. He apparently ran off to Ireland with some of his aunt's mock-heroic friends. At least that's what they say in the bars in Hooley Square."

"Poor woman, that's ghastly."

"Yes, it is. Can you spare tomorrow afternoon, too?"

"I should work on a review that has been giving me trouble. But no, I'll finish that on Sunday. I'd much rather be with you."

"Good. What's the problem you're having?"

"I am almost afraid to tell you. It won't increase your respect for my profession to know that it is riven with controversy over whether people loved each other before—the periodization is disputed too—but, roughly, before about 1550."

"*What? All* people?"

"I thought it would surprise you. The thesis is generally limited to Europe."

"Hmm—1550," he pondered. "Does that mean that the first lovers were middle-class Protestants?"

"One version is very close to that."

"Isn't that what is called counterintuitive?"

"Yes, I find it so; but trendy historians aim at being

perverse. They're always arguing things like emancipa-
tion is bad for minorities or education hurts the poor.
This idea isn't so wildly implausible as some of their
others."

"But, Molly, have the people advancing this argument
read anything written before 1550?"

"Some of them haven't read anything written before
1950. But you've put your finger on my problem.
You've said it all, and I can't think of anything else to
say to fill up the space they're saving for me."

"It boggles the mind. You know Virgil, don't you?"
The inanity of the idea had driven him to his feet as if to
combat it, and he paced the room reciting Book IV.
"And that's comparatively restrained. Do you know
this one?" he asked, proceeding to Catullus as she listened spellbound.

"You do learn to memorize at a Jesuit school," she
said.

"I did not learn that poem in high school."

"No," she agreed. "I suppose you didn't." But she was
thinking: that's it. That's Yeats again, our Billy, right on
the money. She had often thought of "The Scholars" in
connection with Dean Christopher Boggle, his peren-
nially woebegone wife, and hysterical frigidity among
the Sumners. A pedant shuffling, coughing ink . . .
thinking what the others think. As she watched Nick,
she thought, Yes, that must be the way Catullus walked!

"What are you thinking, smiling like that?" he asked.

Could she say? Would he know? "Scholars" was a
minor poem. It wasn't "The Second Coming" or "Among
Schoolchildren."

"I was thinking of the poet I like as much as you like Catullus."

"Who's that?"

"Yeats," she said. "He has a poem about the way Catullus should and should not be read."

He did know because he said, "Why, Molly, you must have kissed the Blarney stone. Will you have enough time if I come at three?"

She had plenty of time but accomplished nothing, the more so because she had read and reread in rage and horror the account in the morning paper of the carnage Friday night in a pub where Catholics and Protestants drank together. It was nearly twelve before she could think of love in any century at all.

Then Ned Perkins called, saying he had come to town unexpectedly, might he have his salmon tonight, or, since it was very short notice, wouldn't she rather have dinner with him? She told him she was busy that evening, would Sunday do as well? No, he intended to go back to his farm late Saturday night. The next time, then.

At 2:30 she laid down her pen in disgust. "And if I use the word 'natural,' I'll be a laughingstock."

They drove to the North Shore. It was far too cold to swim so they walked in the dunes. Eventually they sat on a high hill where they could look at the marsh and the sea.

"How's your review?" Nick asked.

"Not so good. How's your case?"

"Not good either. Do you know any of the Community Mental Health people? She's made it very hot for them; she's been charging that they do abortion referrals."

"No, but Margaret Donahue would know them."

"I'll ask her about it. And what about the Planned Parenthood Clinic itself, the one that Mrs. Putnam supports?"

"That's not in Newnham, it's in Walden. There's just a hot line," Molly said.

"Yes, but Walden is in her district, both the state senate district she currently represents and the congressional one to which she aspires. She has picketed them often, and she is widely believed to have made follow-up calls to girls seen to enter. You know, the phone rings at three in the morning. 'Why did you murder your baby?' "

"I know nothing about the clinic staff. Abortion isn't my issue. I don't think it should be illegal; if a girl is very young, it seems altogether preferable and I think people who persecute after the fact are ghouls. But all that said, honestly, the idea of it horrifies me."

"Does it?"

"Yes. I'm not a Catholic," she felt obliged to add, and it came out sounding defiant.

"Okay." He smiled. "I'll ask Margaret Donahue about social services in Newnham."

"Yes, do. I had lunch with her and Bess Brewster a few days ago, and Margaret knows everything worth knowing about the district."

"She is very central. Has she been getting threatening phone calls?"

"No, she hasn't. Bess asked her that. Do you think it's odd that she hasn't?"

"Not necessarily, though she's probably more influential than either of the others. What did she think of Bess?"

"She was afraid her candidacy might take suburban votes away from Harrigan and make it easier, not harder, for Mary Agnes to win. I think she's probably right. Bess may have to bring her very attractive children into the campaign; but most of them are doing constructive things abroad at the moment."

"Molly, who do you think did it? Assuming that Agatha did not live a secret life we've failed to uncover and that Mary Agnes was the intended victim?"

"The dean of Scattergood College."

"Your dean?"

"Yes, Christopher Boggle."

"Motive?"

"That's easy. He wants to be president of Scattergood."

"Haven't you always had a woman? And doesn't everyone, especially these days, prefer that?"

"Certainly, but if Mary Agnes were out of the race and Bess were elected—mind you, I think you or I, let alone Harrigan, could beat her simply by putting our names on the ballot; but if she hasn't grasped that yet, Boggle wouldn't have a clue—if Bess were elected, Boggle would serve as acting president while a search committee was constituted and while it ground out a short list. And if anyone, anyone at all, objected to those candidates, it could go on for years. Scattergood is a Quaker institution. We try to reach consensus. It took us nearly eighteen months to agree on Bess. And, although she may not be *your* ideal woman . . ."

"No," he said, "she's not." He was thinking how un-affectedly Molly held the wild beach pea and plum blos-soms she had picked. Women often looked so awkward with flowers, florists' flowers at any rate. "But then I wouldn't be her choice either, I suppose."

Molly found it hard to resume her train of thought as she speculated on Nick's ideal woman and mentally con-trasted Bess Brewster, who was not, with that rose or-gandy bridesmaid, Teresa Dellachiesa, who might be. She looked at him blankly.

"You were telling me about the murderous intentions of Mr. Boggle," he said.

"Oh, yes. Bess was a very uncontroversial choice. Un-exceptionable. Her politics are, in the context of Scat-tergood, centrist; she has, and I do not think it was nugatory, a well-connected husband who dotes on her; and her scholarship is sound. It is pedestrian, I think, but it isn't drivel. And the people who really can't stand her—the ones who turn purple when someone says role model (chiefly they are in the so-called high-threshold fields like biochemistry or Chinese, where you have to know a great deal to do anything at all)—most of them have simply given up on college politics and devote them-selves to their students and their research."

"You haven't given up on college politics?"

"No, I think we ought to try and preserve liberal arts; but I assure you that Boggle could rule, if not reign, for years—and eventually they might give him the title, too."

"But you don't think he actually did it? I shouldn't have someone get to work on him?"

"Oh no, I wish I did. But if you *could* prove it, if you could frame Boggle . . ."

"If I framed Boggle for you, what would you do for me?" He looked at her with inviting impropriety.

"If you put Boggle away, you would have the satisfaction of knowing that you had done much for higher education in America."

"It would be churlish not to be content with that."

"It would."

"I'll look forward to it. In the meantime, how do you feel about predestination?" And he began to kiss her in a practiced and purposeful way.

(10)

THE WATERFORD CHANDELIER, an elaborate
cascade of leaded crystal drops, hung directly over the
center of an immense mahogany table; its polished surface shivered under the great weight of light. At one
end of the table, immersed in her work, Mary Agnes
O'Pake sat signing letters. From time to time she slashed
out the typed closing and wrote a more personal conclusion. Invariably she added a handwritten postscript. She
had been at it since seven o'clock, when they finished
dinner; she had begun reading through a stack of weekly
newspapers and noting down the names of people whom
she wanted to congratulate or condole. She interrupted
her work only to answer the telephone on a side table
near her elbow: sometimes her voice was gentle and

commiserating, sometimes shrill with indignation, and, once that evening, it had been hushed and breathless as she answered, "Yes, yes, of course, yes, thank you."

Her father and Officer Driscoll sat in an adjoining parlor. Mr. O'Pake dozed in a reclining chair; Driscoll was watching television and turning around regularly to watch her through the open double doors as she worked. He had often spent Saturday evenings like this, relaxing in the front room while his mother ironed in the kitchen and stacked his neatly folded shirts on the dining room table. Men had started wearing open-necked golf shirts to church, but that departure, like folk masses, was an innovation Driscoll had not embraced. He reflected that many couples in Newnham were doing just what they were doing now: the man watching television, the woman busying herself in another room. It made no difference at all to him that she was writing rather than mending at the dining room table. It felt right to be there with her.

"Want a beer, Tom?" Mr. O'Pake asked when he awoke from his nap.

"No thanks, Pop," he said. Mr. O'Pake had told him to call him that. "I'm on duty."

"Relax, Tom." Mr. O'Pake rose heavily from his chair. "I'll lock up. When you leave, just lock the door to the breezeway behind you." The mortuary, where a cot had been set up for Driscoll, was attached to the house by an enclosed walkway, with bolt-locked doors at either end. "We'll go to the nine at Queen of Heaven. All right with you, Aggie?"

"Yes, Pop." Mary Agnes looked up from her letters.

"If I'm gone when you get up, don't worry. There's a Holy Name breakfast at Catherine of Alexandria, and I may go there instead."

"Yes," he said, "maybe you should. Remember to tell Tom what you decide so he can set his alarm."

"Yes, I will. Good night, Pop."

"Good night, Aggie. Night, Tom."

"Good night, Pop," Driscoll echoed. It seemed like the father-in-law going upstairs to give the couple some privacy. Since he had begun guarding her, they usually watched the eleven o'clock news together.

The senator looked at her watch. It was 10:45. "I have a headache," she announced. "I'm going to my room."

"Don't you want to see the news?"

"I have a set upstairs. They're doing something about Harrigan on Channel Nine. I'll watch that. You can flip between Three and Five. Here—" She handed him a note pad. "Write down anything they say about the campaign. Try to get what they say and who said it. Okay?"

"Sure, I'll be happy to." He was disappointed that she was turning in so early, but pleased to oblige her. He took notes dutifully and then settled down to watch a late movie on cable; Doris Day, surrounded by daffodils, was singing "Once I had a secret love that lived within the heart of me . . ." when Driscoll heard a noise outside. The senator slept at the back of the house; a fire escape, put in when seven girls slept on the top floors of the big house, led down from her room into the garden. Driscoll thought an inner room would be safer—Agatha's old bedroom with one tiny window would have been

94

ideal—but Mary Agnes liked the room she had, and since the fire stairs could be raised and secured at the first landing, he had done that rather than inconvenience her.

Driscoll's gun belt lay on the parlor coffee table; instantly he reached forward and took his revolver from it. He checked the cartridge chamber as he had been taught to do, then made his way to the kitchen and out through the back door. He had not been imagining the noise; he heard it clearly now. Driscoll had never fired the gun except on the target range; he had only rarely in the line of duty removed it from its holster. Now he clasped it hard; the handle filled his sweating palm and cooled it. He pressed himself into a rose of Sharon tree by the kitchen door and peered through its leaves: a slight figure, wearing oxfords, slacks, a heavy Aran turtleneck sweater, and a tweed cap, was moving along the lower landing of the fire escape, moving away from the senator's bedroom window, not toward it.

"Jesus, I'm too late . . ." He sprang forward as the figure dropped lightly to the ground. He caught the intruder roughly and was immediately turned upon and slapped hard across the mouth. The senator's reflexes were quicker than his own, but he did not relax his grip.

"Where were you going?" he asked Mary Agnes sternly. "You know I'm responsible for you."

"I'll be safer where I'm going than I was at the Athenaeum with you," she said.

"Where do you want to go at this hour?" He was pleading with her, though his words were firm. "I can't let you go off alone at night. What would your father say? What would the governor say?"

She told him whom she was meeting. His face fell. "Didn't you know you could trust me? Me?" he repeated, his voice hoarse with distress. "You know where I stand."

"I promised I'd come alone."

"I won't let you go alone."

"I have to," she said.

"No." He was adamant. "But if you want me to stay outside once we get there, I guess that'd be all right."

She relented. "We'll take my car. I'm supposed to park in the lot by the bowling alley across from Saint John the Evangelist and walk from there. You know the way?"

"I know some back ways," he said.

She handed him the keys. They got into the car, and he released the handbrake, letting the car roll noiselessly down the driveway in neutral. He did not start the engine until they were well clear of the house and he was certain they were alone on the street. Mary Agnes smiled approvingly.

Nick and Molly talked during dinner in the desultory manner of couples long acquainted. They had kissed for a long time in the dunes and, as they drove back to the city, Molly waited with ebbing composure for the next move.

"I had a great line, Molly."

"Let's hear it."

"Do you want to come up and see my vernacular Bible?"

"That is a great line, but why 'had'?"

"Because I've decided not to use it."

"Oh?" He had, nonetheless, stopped in front of his place.

"I think it would be inauspicious."

"Inauspicious?" she asked softly.

"Not a good beginning for us. It matters too much, to both of us, Molly, for this to be a fling. Come inside. Let's talk this over."

His flat was on the top floor of a well-kept triple-decker. "My father didn't trust banks or corporations," Nick explained as they climbed the oiled hardwood staircase. "He put all his savings into real estate. This is the second building he bought. My mother still lives in our old house, with my older sister and her family."

The living room they entered was sparsely furnished, its walls hung with pictures and posters. Nick turned on a light, and Molly saw that one of the posters announced the 1946 referendum held to determine whether Italy should be a republic or a monarchy. Automatically, she stepped forward to read the fine print.

"Read that some other time, would you? I want to talk with you now. You feel the same, don't you? We love each other or we will soon."

"Nick," she said, sitting down next to him on the sofa, "you appeal to me very much."

"I don't want to appeal to you," he said angrily. "I want to marry you. Oh, not tonight, not next Thursday. I'm not a total anachronism. But I want you to know that I am serious about this. I want you to take it seriously, too."

"Nick, this is very premature. Not," she faltered, "because I don't care for you, but because I do. You scarcely know me. You probably already know women who would be better for you."

"Better for me? Are you thinking about the girl I was dancing with? Do you know her?"

"Not her, perhaps, but someone like her."

"Like her in what way?"

"In many ways you will eventually prefer," Molly replied steadily, "whatever you may feel for me now."

"That is ridiculous. Molly, I have done nothing to encourage Teresa to think I care for her."

"You've only to walk through the door to encourage any woman alive."

"You're not so bad yourself. I don't know how much you caught of what was said while we were playing *bocce*."

"Not much. My Italian is mostly scholarly."

"None of that was. But let me finish about Teresa. She's a sweet young woman, but much too pious. I've never tasted her *vitello tonnato*, but it can't be as good as yours. Moreover, she is a very bad *bocce* player. And my mother doesn't approve of her. She thinks Teresa doesn't have the strength of character to cope with teenagers, especially, she says, if my sons are anything like me."

"I'm thirty-one."

"So we won't have six kids. Molly, I'm a reasonable man."

"Nick, I think people are, in general—there are exceptions—happier . . ."

"With people of similar backgrounds? Molly, I'm prepared to hear that you aren't sure, but don't descend to pop sociology. There's not a dime's worth of difference between us, about anything either of us seriously cares about or believes in."

Molly turned away from him and he drew her back. She did not resist but said, unyieldingly, "I believe you would be happier with someone else. I wish I didn't think so, but I do."

"Molly, what do you take me for? This is insulting." He paused. "What's driving you to answer me with clichés?"

"Clichés sometimes capture something."

"Of course they do, and this one *is* autobiographical, isn't it? Because if it isn't based on experience, I don't know where you're getting it. Molly, we don't have to tell each other everything, but there was someone, like you superficially, who once told me that I appealed to her but not enough. That's why I was furious when you said that. But she was someone who thought of Al Capone where you would think of Galileo. Everyone must have had experiences like that."

"Yes, it's a free country. Love makes strange bedfellows."

"I read a lot of Yeats," he said.

"Yeats can get you through anything," Molly recalled. " 'A pity beyond all telling / Is hid in the heart of love.' "

"Yes, there's no other modern poet like him, though Kathleen—that was her name, and it was years ago—preferred Browning."

"Which Browning?" Molly wanted to know.

"Mrs. Browning."

"You proposed marriage to someone who preferred

Elizabeth Barrett Browning to Yeats? That's shocking."

Nick, much heartened, began gaily to reassure her. "I was very young. I only did it once—that is, repeatedly, pathetically, but to only one woman. I'll never do it again. And I'd forgive you anything. Molly, don't cry. Yours hurt much worse, didn't it? It involved things worse than prejudice—real conviction and real betrayal?"

"You are very perceptive." Yes, it had involved the very idea of conviction, of commitments based on knowledge and sympathy, rather than on blood. She had gotten to know Dan in a seminar on the Enlightenment; he had sung her that Yiddish song *Komme hier, mein philosophe*. "Nick," she resumed deliberately, "I think that whatever convictions people consciously uphold there are still fears, atavisms, affinities . . ."

"There is absolutely nothing wanting in our affinities. I thought I had begun to convince you of that. But that wasn't the problem last time, was it?"

"No, it wasn't."

"Then," he said, taking her onto his lap, "that's all the more reason we should be promised to each other first. Oh, don't cry, Molly, please don't. Or maybe you should, for a little while." He understood what it meant for her to abandon herself in his arms to the memory of some terrible sorrow. He held her close against him and neither of them spoke until the phone rang.

"Oh damn, I've got to answer it. I'm sorry," he said. "Remember, Molly, 'the pity beyond all telling,' whatever it was, it's over now. It's finished." He kept an arm around her, consoling, determined, as he reached for the telephone. "Hello. Yes. Oh, my God. Where? When? Both dead? Good, that's something. I'll get there as soon as I can." He hung up. "It appears that, this time, some-one has managed to kill Senator O'Pake. A hit-and-run, half an hour ago in South Boston. The trooper who was with her is still alive, but barely."

"What was she doing in Southie at one in the morning?"

"That's one of the first things I'll try to find out. The commissioner has just gone to break the news to the governor. Are you all right? I'll take you home when-ever you're ready."

"I'm ready to go right now," Molly said with an ef-fort. "It must be very urgent that you get there." She said nothing more as he drove her home and she leapt from the car almost before he had stopped in front of her house.

He raced after her. "This is urgent, too, or I wouldn't have spoken tonight so abruptly. Think it over. But in kindness to me, don't deliberate too long. I've got a pretty good idea of your feelings. I don't want them sicklied o'er."

(11)

IT HAD HAPPENED too late to get into the Sunday papers, but the radio and television news spoke of little else. Mary Agnes O'Pake had been killed instantly; the state trooper accompanying her was in surgery for internal injuries, was reported to be in critical condition, in guarded condition, was expected to live. The senator's sister had been killed in a tragic accident the previous week. And were these accidents? Could the public be asked to accept these outrages as coincidence? What were the police doing? The governor, meeting reporters as he left twelve o'clock mass, said he would not rest, nor would he permit any law enforcement officer to rest, until justice had been done.

Nick called to say he'd been up all night and was going home to have a nap while he waited for the results of some preliminary lab work. Could he see her briefly in the early evening?

Molly had been awake most of the night, too, incredulous: happiness could not come so easily; there must be a catch. When Nick arrived, he held her fast for a few minutes. "You feel uncertain," he said finally, releasing her, "but not unwilling."

"You're nearly always right about people, aren't you?"

"Generally," he said, "so far."

"And what about the murder?" she asked.

"*That*," he said, "baffles me. It almost could have been an accident. There isn't much to go on. A little paint and broken glass . . ."

"What color paint?"

"Black, highly polished, with good wax; not the spray kind. The hand-rubbed sort you use with a chamois."

"Some sort of official car?"

"I was privileged to be present when that was suggested to the governor."

"What did he say?"

"Nothing I would wish you to hear."

"Nick, I'm not . . ."

"Not somebody in a fresco gazing with infinite forbearance at the instruments with which you were done in? Do you really think I'd find that a virtue?"

There was no reply to that, so she pursued the question of the car. "It was a well-kept car, well maintained, someone would notice that it was gone?"

"Yes, unless its owner was on vacation. Nothing's been reported stolen. It might, I suppose, be some sort of vehicle that isn't used on weekends—or its owner may be the culprit—or it may have been used and returned . . ."

"What about the damage? Would it need body work?"

"We hope that will turn up something. But it's just as likely it won't. We know it lost some paint and more than one headlight—but the sort of actual denting would depend on where the impact occurred, and that is difficult to determine from the injuries."

"You know, Nick, when those all-night, coin-operated car washes opened up, the first thing that occurred to me was that someone could come in after an accident and wash the blood and hair off his car with four quarters."

"That's a good idea." He went over to the phone.

"Dave, have we looked into car washes? No, the U-Wash-It type. Yes, let's. Thanks. Have you turned up anything about Bill Foley? No, I'll be at this number a little longer. Let me give it to you. Now"—he sat down beside Molly—"let's suppose that the car was used by an owner or with his consent or returned to the owner unscathed."

"Lots of people keep touch-up paint for their cars. I have some myself in the glove compartment."

"They do. And you don't have to be a mechanic to replace a headlight. I don't know if you've ever noticed—there are just a few screws; anybody who had the part and a Phillips screwdriver could do it in three minutes."

"And if someone had, well, an official car—or say several such cars—wouldn't he be likely to be prepared to do that?"

"Sure. It would depend on how accommodating or how crooked the nearest body shop was."

She thought about this.

"I still don't see how a woman like Mary Agnes, who never went anywhere without that entourage of flunkies, could have gone to Southie alone in the middle of the night."

"Everyone down there would recognize her. She'd be no more likely to be mugged than the Madonna; besides, she wasn't alone. Driscoll was with her. I found his revolver locked in the glove compartment of her car parked a few blocks from the intersection where they were run down."

"But Driscoll isn't able to say anything yet, is he?" Molly asked.

"No, he's not—and from a humanitarian point of view, it's a good thing there's physical grounds to sedate him. He'd never accept medication and I don't think he could stand it otherwise. You saw him at the Athenaeum."

"Yes, I did. But surely he hadn't been guarding her alone for a week?"

"No, the State Police gave their fullest attention to her security, as you might imagine. Her itineraries were checked like nobody's since the pope, and there were always two men on duty besides Driscoll, except of course when she was asleep and the burglar alarm, which her father had installed some time ago, had been set and checked and rechecked. Driscoll still slept in the mortuary, though. She liked him and relied on his advice. He mentioned that to me on Friday. I don't think anything in his life had ever made him prouder."

"I've seen Mary Agnes teaching ignorant men violent ways."

"It wasn't like that at all. He didn't enter into any of her really savage enthusiasms—he may have been one of very few men who ever saw her as a woman who needed protection—you know, a good woman, in something a little over her head, but he was going to do his damnedest to get her through it and beat up the guys who had scared her if he could find them."

"Nick, I love the breadth of your sympathies."

"Sure, baby, *nihil humanum* . . ."

"Then you think she confided in him about—whatever she was doing, and he went along—either agreeing she should go, or because he couldn't let her go alone?"

"Yes, or he saw her leave and followed her. I'll try to clear that up when he's conscious and his doctors think he can talk about it . . . though when that will be . . ."

The phone rang. "It's for you," she said.

"Ryan's vanished," he said as he hung up.

"Who's Ryan?"

"One of the entourage, Mary Agnes's most recent gofer and amanuensis. There have been many before him, but he's the best she's had in years. Her office had been looking for him all day Saturday, and we joined in after the accident."

"And he's missing?"

"Yes, and there'd been difficulties between them for some time—he'd been taking time off—still doing the work of two or three regular men, but not eating and sleeping in the office. He hasn't been seen since he closed the campaign headquarters in Hooley Square at ten on Friday night, and nobody knows where to find him."

"I can't place him."

"You wouldn't remember him. He's the sort you

don't see; he gets lost among all the 'Ivy Day in the Committee Room' types."

"Ivy Day. That is it precisely. The trivialization of history. The profanation of memory. And I would bet she had never heard of Parnell, or Joyce. Do you like Joyce?"

"*Dubliners* is brilliant. And *Portrait*, of course. Everybody at my school read that. I don't like *Ulysses* much. Is that the look of encouraging inquiry you give students when you want them to elaborate? It's convincing. I really feel it, that you want to hear what I think about *Ulysses*."

"I do, believe me."

"Parts of it are excellent, Molly-my-girl, but I like the old *Odyssey* better."

"So do I. Anybody'd be glad if you washed up on her beach and stayed for a while. I certainly would be."

"But you're not just any nymph. You're Penelope. Not, to clear up anything from Sociology 100 that may still be troubling you, the part about remaining at home, but the other attributes—brains, resolution, steadfast love. I'll call you in the morning. Will you be here?"

"Yes," she said, "I'll be weaving."

Molly stayed up all night and wrote a scathingly intemperate review. She had just come back from posting it express mail when Nick called with the news.

"Ryan's back."

"Really? Good for you. How did you find him?"

"I didn't. He was there to open up the office at seven-thirty this morning."

"Where had he been?"

"He claimed he'd been in Falmouth—the senator had told him weeks ago not to schedule anything for her this weekend—and he had wanted to be alone, to think, or so he said. He hadn't turned on the television once all weekend and, although he ate out on Saturday, he never left the room at all, except to go to early mass on Sunday, until he checked out to drive back to Boston at dawn today."

"Do you believe him?"

"He checked in and out when he said he did. Of course, he could have driven back and forth to South Boston—she was killed not far from the Southeast Expressway—a dozen times."

"Was he alone?"

"The people at the motel think he was. It's a respectable place. The maid found nothing to indicate he hadn't been alone."

"And she would know?"

"I think we can assume so. He left the place neat, she said, so he may have done any sort of cleaning up after himself before he left. The only trace of him she remembered finding was a large Dunkin' Donuts box and an empty gallon container of milk—both of which he said he'd bought after church so he wouldn't have to go out again."

"And he really hadn't heard about her death?"

"He seemed genuinely thunderstruck to me."

"Doesn't he have a car radio?"

"It's broken. He hasn't had time to have it fixed."

"And he wouldn't have seen it in the Sunday papers."

"No. It's a lame story, the weekend in a motel meditating and eating doughnuts. I can't believe he couldn't make up a better one if he needed to."

"Is he clever enough to reckon on your thinking that, rather than striving for verisimilitude himself?"

"He is smarter than he thinks he is, odd guy; but that seems a little too artful."

"Was Ryan at the Athenaeum, too, the night the other sister was killed?"

"Yes, he said he wanted to see in person how Mrs. Brewster worked a crowd. And there was a rumor about a liberal Republican he thought he could check at the same time."

"Sounds plausible," Molly said, "except for the part about the Republican. Are you going to be working late tonight?"

"Very late, unfortunately."

"Come over when you've finished; we'll have a midnight supper and talk over the case."

"Is that what you like to do at night, hypothesize?"

"I'll be open to other suggestions."

"Expect me around eleven thirty."

Dr. Brewster was now seriously worried about his wife's safety and asked Nick to lunch with him at his club. He hoped it would be convenient, he said; it was about equidistant between Children's Hospital and police headquarters. And it was, Nick thought—geographically. "Thank you, Dr. Brewster, I'd like very much to have lunch with you."

"Lieutenant Hannibal," he said as they were seated, "I'm concerned about my wife."

"Yes, sir, I should think you would be. She told me about the calls."

"Yesterday, the campus police picked up a man, hiding very close to the jogging path my wife always takes. It's impossible entirely to protect the campus of a women's college from voyeurs and exhibitionists. And few of them, as you must know better than I, are in fact dangerous. But the young women are gone. Commencement was three weeks ago."

"The local flashers may not be acquainted with the academic calendar."

"That's true, and somewhat reassuring, but this one was armed."

"Armed? The Scattergood police don't carry guns, do they?"

"No. The trustees won't hear of it. Bess is very opposed, and I've never seen the need for it myself. The man who noticed him summoned assistance and the two of them very courageously subdued him and turned him over to the town police."

"I'm glad you told me about this. They hadn't notified us. I'll check into it right away."

"There may be no connection at all, but it troubles me. What I'm most inclined to do," Brewster confided, "is to take Bess to Geneva."

"A very safe city in a very safe country," Nick agreed.

"Yes, but it will take time. I have a standing offer at a research institute that I'd like to take up, if I could only get something for Bess at WHO. You understand, my wife is very capable, very—a man doesn't like to brag—

much sought after. I can fix it, but it will take time. Scotty's only just been confirmed."

"Confirmed, sir?" Nick did not like to think of himself as parochial, but what was this? Did Episcopalians not undertake new jobs, or would it be, not accept political appointments, for a period of time following their children's confirmation? He was at a loss.

"I beg your pardon, Lieutenant Hannibal. My wife says I am too elliptical. A very old friend of ours, my prep school roommate—thinks the world of Bess—has just been made Deputy Undersecretary for International Organizations. I know how intent he will be on getting Bess to do something for the World Health Organization. She is keenly interested in protecting midwives from physicians in developing countries. I fear I have been indiscreet."

"Certainly not, sir. I shall look forward to news of the appointment."

"Thank you. I fear I am old-fashioned as well as indiscreet."

"I'd feel exactly as you do," Nick replied.

"Are you married yourself?" Brewster asked, noting the warmth with which Nick spoke.

"Not yet."

"I hope you will have that happiness before too long. I've enjoyed our talk very much. What do you suggest I do in the meantime?"

"Maintain the surveillance, exercise ordinary prudence, sleep lightly. We think that Senator O'Pake was lured to her death by a phone call; but she was, unlike your wife, a naive woman in many ways."

"Yes, that's true and again most reassuring. You'll come again?"

"Certainly, sir, with pleasure."

Sister Jude answered her telephone.

"Sister, this is Liz Putnam, Liz Hennessy Putnam. I wanted to talk to you. Perhaps you don't remember me?"

"I remember you perfectly." A girl of chilling rectitude, she would return a nickel to the lunchroom if she'd been given too much change, a tall, plain girl with large, all-seeing, uncompromising eyes, eyes that were never averted. Lizzie was a good girl; and Sister Jude had said so, rather sharply, to His Eminence. The Putnams had got themselves a fresh shot of Puritanism when they got her.

"I have been involved, since I left Holy Sepulchre, with family planning. And I have been very much at odds with Senator O'Pake. I remembered that she was, I am sorry to say I've forgotten precisely how, a relative of yours."

"Not a close one. Her sister is my brother's widow."

"I see. I did want you to know that I am sorry and that I'm sure, that I'm making *very* sure, that none of my associates knows anything whatsoever about her tragic death."

"I don't think anyone supposes they do."

"It's very good of you to say that, but I wanted to assure you personally that I would send anyone who did to the police, instantly."

"I am sure you would." So fast their teeth would rattle, but you'd go with them and get them a lawyer.

"Mrs. Putnam, we do differ, but no one who ever knew you, certainly not I who taught you, could think for a minute . . ."

"Please call me 'Lizzie.' And you, you yourself are not bereaved?"

"Frankly, no. I grieve for her no more than I would for any soul."

"I'm glad, because I am *so* sorry. Someone told my father-in-law—I shouldn't say who, but I am sure you can guess—what the cardinal said about you and the school when I was elected to head Planned Parenthood. The Putnams all thought it was a stitch, but I thought it must have been horrid for you. You made such an impression on me. My mother and my aunts never did anything but agree with their husbands or pretend to. You were the first independent woman I ever knew. I believe that what I am doing is right, but I was so distressed that it made problems for you. I meant to write you then."

"It is good of you to call."

"Thank you, Sister. I *am* sorry."

A "stitch," "horrid," "so distressed." The vocabulary had changed, but obviously the girl had not. "God love you, Lizzie," she said.

(1 2)

"THIS IS DELICIOUS, Molly. Do you have a whole repertoire of cold soups?" Nick had managed to get away earlier than he'd expected and was tasting the soup in the kitchen while she sliced a dish of tomatoes. The pleasantness of the domesticity into which they were quickly falling was working upon her.

"Considering the job market in history, I thought I ought to have other arrows in my quiver. Open the wine, would you? And tell me how the investigation is progressing."

"Harrigan has his usual embarrassment of alibis."

"Really?" she asked as she served the soup. "His devoted wife?"

"No, she is traveling in Ireland with her parents. But that hasn't simplified his social life much. It does raise an interesting possibility about cars, though. His absent father-in-law owns Mulcahy Cadillac-Olds. He makes most of his money these days in used cars, but he still sells, leases, and lends, to friends in the public eye, luxurious, heavy, exclusively American-made . . ."

"Black sedans," Molly finished the thought.

"White and silver are available too, though they are passing out of fashion. Mulcahy owns a multitude of the sort of car we are looking for."

"I saw Harrigan myself today."

"You did? Where?"

"At O'Pake election headquarters. I went there this afternoon to see if any of her people might be willing to work for Bess. He must have had the same idea. He was talking with Ryan when I arrived."

"Had they reached an agreement?"

"I don't think so, but Harrigan must have made him an offer because as Ryan was leaving Harrigan told him to think it over."

"Anything else?" Nick asked.

"Yes, I thought Ryan was rather curt with him. He certainly didn't seem grateful."

"He's a very deferential sort ordinarily."

"Yes, he looks as if he would be. That's what struck me about the contempt he showed for Harrigan, who was oozing bonhomie."

"Ryan's manner wasn't accusatory? He didn't seem to blame Harrigan for the senator's death?"

"Oh, no, something far short of that. More like dirty tricks. It did occur to me that Harrigan might have made him a less open offer earlier on."

"Such as?" he asked.

"You know the practice of planting someone in a rival campaign?"

"Someone who is disobliging to the press and keeps messing up the scheduling?"

"Yes, and giving bad advice about a constituency he's supposed to be able to deliver. Harrigan probably asked Ryan to do some of those things and promised him a more dignified role after the primary."

"Do you expect Harrigan to win the primary?"

"I don't know. I hope not. Bess, with all her shortcomings, would be an infinitely more responsible legislator."

"You don't think much of Harrigan?"

"Nick, I think he's the worst sort of opportunistic swinger."

"But he doesn't strike you as a man who's going places?"

"No, he does not. He's too self-absorbed to notice what other people are like. Or he wouldn't make demeaning proposals to a man like Ryan, who anyone would see is incorruptible."

"You don't know that he did."

"No, but I strongly sense it. And you need not say what you are about to say about intuition; when men have it, it's called 'acumen.' Harrigan lacks it, and people without it go nowhere in politics, never have, never will."

"Harrigan likes to win."

"Who doesn't? Nick, he's smarmy and vain, but I cannot believe he's stupid enough to undertake a gratuitous and easily detected crime."

"It may turn out to be neither gratuitous nor easily proved," he said testily.

"Nick, what's troubling you? Let's have coffee in the living room. Come sit next to me."

"Did Harrigan make a pass at you?"

"He asked me to have a drink with him, and I did because I wanted to find out how he was planning to run. I was sure all he wanted from me was similar intelligence about Bess."

"I doubt that very much."

"In any case, I thought I could extract more from him than I'd divulge myself."

"And that was it? Oh hell, I know I've no right to ask you that."

"You have every right, but no reason . . . That wasn't it. I told him I was busy tonight and every night until the primary and that immediately thereafter I was leaving for Florence."

"He had enough acumen to get that, I hope."

"I think so. When is his wife coming back?" Molly asked.

"Next week. Are you really staying until September?"

"Yes, I promised Bess I would and there's a mass of published material I should read through before I start work in the archives. I want to stay until things are settled here."

Nick put down his cup and took hers from her. "Are you ready to settle something now?"

"Nick, I'm yours for the taking."

"That isn't what I asked you. Will you at least think about marrying me?"

"Nick, I don't think you would be happy with me."

"You are a liberal, aren't you? I am an adult. Don't you think I'm the best judge of things promoting my own happiness?"

"Touché," she acknowledged.

"Come then, dearest, why not?"

She could not speak for a few minutes and then, chokingly, began, "I don't think . . . I cannot believe you'll keep on loving me."

Nothing, he concluded, is bad enough for the guy who's responsible for this. This is going to take longer than I thought. "It's going to rain soon," he said. "Let's go for a walk. I'll show you the path I used to take down to the trolley to get to school, along the railroad tracks. It's full of urban wild flowers and broken bottles."

"Sounds idyllic," she said, welcoming the change of topic. "It's wonderful the way city children can find wilderness anywhere."

"Yes, and when the rain starts there are old shelters from the time it was a regular commuter line."

"Did you take girls to them, to make out?"

"I did; they're placed at very convenient intervals."

"Will you hold my hand as we walk?"

"I'll start by holding your hand," he said as they went out. "There's an order one follows. Do you want to hear about Harrigan's father-in-law? He goes to Ireland several times a year."

"Goodness, he must be lots more ethnic than the boy mayor."

"He doesn't spend all his time at the Abbey Theater. We think he's involved with Eirelief. You know about them?"

"Yes, they collect money ostensibly to support widows and orphans and families of detainees; but mostly they buy arms."

"They do some of each; but I imagine Mulcahy is more interested in munitions than hot lunches."

"That would embarrass Harrigan, wouldn't it? He's awfully upscale."

"Yes, but no one could reasonably hold him accountable for his father-in-law's politics, and some people might like him better for it."

"Mary Agnes must have known Mulcahy," Molly said. The rain began softly.

"I'm certain she did. And if they fell out over something, Harrigan may not be involved at all. Mulcahy could have arranged for an accident to take place in his absence. Or one of his cars could have been used without his consent. Anything's possible there because given the driving habits of his associates, regardless of their public stands on drunk driving, the leased and lent cars are in almost continual disrepair. I sent a man out to see if any of their cars had been damaged over the weekend, and they showed him fifteen." It was raining harder now.

"It comes as no surprise. Is this one of the shelters you spoke of?"

"It is. We can stay here till the rain stops."

They watched the sky clear. Clouds covered and uncovered the moon again and again, until stars were visible too. "The stars seem brighter than they usually do in the city," Molly said.

"We see more clearly down here near the tracks. The embankment shuts out the distracting artificial light."

"You have to be in the shadows to see the light?" she asked.

"Sometimes. You're interested in light imagery, aren't you?"

"Yes, it's central to most of my heresies."

"*O luce magis dilecta.*" He whispered it persuasively. She did remember that line. "Oh, dearer to me than light," she repeated.

"It struck me the first time I read the *Aeneid.*"

"It struck me sometime later," she said.

They left the shelter and began to walk again.

"Are you confident," she asked as they made their way back along the tracks, "that the Harrigan-Mulcahy connection leads somewhere?"

"No, I'm not, and the more I think about it the less I think Harrigan's involved. We didn't find anything useful about the murder weapon at Mulcahy's; but the man I sent, a very sharp kid, thought to look for Mary Agnes's missing driver and found him. I told you about Billy Foley, whom Mary Agnes had fired."

"Yes, nasty gossip about him, you said."

"And it gets seamier all the time."

"Couldn't it be simple? Maybe she just caught him stealing."

"She had already fired him, even before the first murder."

"Maybe she fired him for something else and he stole to get even. Or maybe he was afraid that in addition to firing him she would bring charges against him. Didn't you say there was talk about one of the Moran girls? He might have had some sort of hold over her so that she was reluctant to prosecute him, but he still couldn't be sure that she wouldn't."

"Possibly. But it isn't clear any money is missing. Ryan kept good records. And the books balance. Of course, no one knows what might have come in in cash in violation of campaign finance laws. Ryan has promised me a list of out-of-state contributors."

"I'd be interested to see it," Molly said. "I don't think there would be any conflict of interest now that the candidate is dead. There's no limit, you know, to what one can give in support of an issue, rather than a candidate. Her campaign may have attracted that sort of money."

"I'd be grateful if you would."

"And if I can't make anything of the list, I know someone who can. I have a friend who works for the National Conference of Catholic Bishops and keeps track of the Moral Majority."

"You have friends in curious places. Is he a good friend?"

"He went to Notre Dame with my cousin Tim. He is, as you once said of someone else, too pious."

"Fine. Why don't you consult him? I'm going to be busy all day tomorrow. I'll send you the list. Will you be at home?"

"Yes, I'll be there all day. I get more done at home. If I'm in my office at Scattergood, even after term, people keep dropping in to chat."

"Could I drop in to chat about the list tomorrow night? Just for a half hour or so, I'll have had dinner. I'd like to see you before the night shift. Here we are."

They had arrived at the steps that went back up to the street. "You see, it's just two blocks from your house."

"I'm David Levinson, Professor Rafferty," the young man said.

"I'm Molly," she corrected instinctively.

"Nick asked me to drop this off. It's the list of out-of-state contributions to the O'Pake campaign."

"Thank you so much. Won't you come in? Were there any he particularly wanted to know about?"

"Yes, there are a couple. Some of them have called to ask how the investigation is going. They sound as though they hope they have a martyr." He was a pale, finely made boy with strongly marked dark eyebrows, judiciously rather than fluently well-spoken.

"Won't you tell me about it? I think Nick has decided I am sufficiently clear of suspicion to discuss the case with."

"Oh, yes, he said you've been very helpful."

"Would you like some coffee?"

"Yes, thank you. If it's not too much trouble."

"None at all."

She went off, taking the list with her. When she returned with the coffee, he was standing in front of her bookshelf.

"You're interested in history?" she asked.

"I'm interested in the Holocaust."

"Interested in resistance too?" she said encouragingly.

"Yes, but I wish there had been more of it."

"So do I. But reprisals weren't just a risk, they were a certainty. People must have been tormented by the fear that they would do more harm than good."

"That's what Nick says, no dumb heroics."

"Have you been working with him long?"

"It seems a long time to me, since I was arrested two years ago."

"How did you happen to be arrested?" Molly asked, careful to suppress her astonishment. This was a deadly earnest young man, with a somewhat defensive formality, not hostile but reserved. It was impossible to imagine him doing anything that warranted his arrest.

"I was resisting arrest," he said, adding with a wry pride, "I was forcibly subdued."

"Were you? It must have been something you felt justified in doing."

"It was, then. I had just joined the Jewish Defense League. It was my first time out with them. Have you heard of them?"

"Of course."

"I guess you don't sympathize with them?"

"I do sympathize. I don't agree. It isn't every man for himself *here*."

"Nick doesn't approve of them at all. He has hundreds of reasons for not taking the law into your own hands. After I was arrested he asked me if I'd like to be a policeman. It was my first offense. Nick and the lawyer my mother got for me fixed it up so it wouldn't go to trial, and Nick arranged for me to take the entrance exam for the police academy. The JDL lawyer wanted me to fight the charge."

"What did you want to do?"

"I wanted to fight it too, but my mother . . ." He would say nothing disloyal. "She'd been through a lot . . ."

"Do you regret it?"

"No. Not very often anyway. It's great to work with Nick. But I get sick of procedure, and going through channels. They keep trying to recruit me for the white-collar crime task force. You know what that means? Auditing . . ." He broke off, struck dumb by the horror of it.

This dear kid, Molly thought, he's aching for conspicuous gallantry and they're asking him to do sums in his head. "What does Nick say about the accounting task force?"

"He tells personnel he needs me in homicide."

Molly heard footsteps running up her front stairs. "I think that's Nick now." And she went quickly to answer the door.

"I've missed you all day," he said. "I had to see you. I can't stay long."

"David's here," she said. "He came with the list."

"Oh, hi, Dave," he said.

David left as soon as he decently could, though they both urged him to stay.

"Have you looked over the list?"

"Yes, briefly," she said, angry even to think of some of the people on it. "What a crew. God, I hate those laissez-faire theocrats. They are abominable."

"Didn't anyone ever tell you intellectual hatreds are the worst? But you're right. People eager to dictate morals ought to enforce just prices too. Banning books and licensing greed is the worst of both worlds. Some of them are good for more than they're down for, wouldn't you think?"

"I'm sure they are. I'll check this out with my friend Peter later."

"Your man with our bishops?"

"Not my man, not my bishops," she said. "We all live in uneasy relation with our pasts. Nick, how did David come to be working with you? He said you helped him after he was arrested. But how did you know him?"

"I recognized his name after the fracas. He had been a witness to an earlier unsolved crime, something that happened while I was in Europe. There was a holdup in his family's drugstore. Two men shot and killed his older brother and wounded his father, who's alive but paraplegic as a result."

"How awful," Molly said. "And he was there? He saw it?"

"That's the really bad part. His brother had managed to push him down beneath the counter before the shooting started. David was frightened and disoriented and he could not identify the suspects. The police weren't sure they had the right men. Maybe they hadn't. Anyway, David agonized over it, asked to see the lineup again and again, reliving it each time; but he could not, in good conscience, say he recognized anyone."

"And so he felt he had failed his father and his brother twice," Molly said. "He did nothing to save them and he could not even help convict their attackers. How old was he?"

"Thirteen, and even before the holdup he had been preoccupied with violence. He's read everything I've ever heard of about the Second World War."

"That's not uncommon. And it's always the most scrupulous boys who take that on—very hard on everyone, especially themselves." Molly recalled several young men she had taught as a graduate student. "Were his grandparents refugees?"

"No, his grandfathers were both born in Boston, in Mattapan actually. And they were military age in the forties, but one was 4-F; he had severe asthma and worked as a bookkeeper at the Naval Yard. The other was deferred because he was a foreman in a small factory that made officers' overcoats."

"I'm sure both of them were invaluable, but from David's point of view, it could scarcely have been worse."

"I tell him from time to time American logistics won the war."

"That's what he needs to hear, but how he must hate the thought. The past is," she said, shuddering, "a 'nightmare pressing on the brain of the living.' "

"Whose line is that? It's not very inventive."

"Marx," she said. "Part of the 'once as tragedy, once as farce,' discussion of historic fiascoes. I think, especially about Ireland, but in general too, that it isn't just a sequence, that preoccupation with tragedy actually engenders farce."

"Funny, I always think of farce preceding tragedy."

"Really, how?"

"Mussolini preceding Hitler," he said shortly.

"Oh, Nick, there's no connection. Ten years of relatively uneventful Italian fascism may have made the democracies a little more nonchalant about Hitler's accession, but it's inconceivable they would have roused themselves to do anything even if it hadn't. Did that trouble you, as a boy?"

"No, no, it didn't, because my father had been a hero." Nick went over to the open window facing the street. The air was still and hot, leaves, dull in the heavy air, hung listlessly. Molly followed him there and laid her head on his shoulder.

"Nick, how did your father die? Would you rather not tell me about it?"

"No, you will appreciate the irony. My father left Italy in 1930, when he was sixteen. He wasn't an educated man; the heroic stories he used to tell me about the Risorgimento were folktales, not history. He found work here as a mechanic and married. He enlisted, right after Pearl Harbor. He was made a master sergeant in North Africa and eventually crossed from Sicily to Naples, just like Garibaldi. He was decorated after the fall of Monte Cassino and marched on to Rome."

"Red shirts vanquishing black shirts," she said. "That's glorious."

"Of course it wasn't Italian Fascists he was fighting. The Germans sent in the varsity when the Americans arrived," he said in a tone of flat bitterness she had heard before, but never in him.

"It was a good fight to win," she said firmly, "as satisfying as myth."

"Yes, I think he felt that it was. And he came through it all—you know how savage the fighting was—entirely unscathed. I was born after the war. You weren't in Massachusetts in the early sixties, were you?"

"No, I wasn't."

"There was a series of what the papers call gangland

slayings in Newnham. Very inglorious." His words came calmly and readily. It sounded like a story he had told himself many times, a story he had taught himself to tell because he could not bear the grief unless he subdued it with conscious irony. "The crux of the disagreement was coin-operated laundries, just within the penumbra of organized crime, so that the killings were not as professional as they should have been. Not formulaic executions, but shots fired from a car. My father was one of the passersby who was hit. He did not linger. It was all over before I got home from school. I was stupefied because his relations with violence had been, up till then, as you said, so frankly satisfying. I couldn't believe it, not for hours afterwards."

"Oh," Molly said, "oh, my love."

"My mother was remarkable. Fatalistic, I suppose. It was an accident. It was over. Bad things happen. She treated it matter-of-factly; he had been killed, but somehow not diminished by it, because she insisted on the utter blindness of chance. My earlier sense of my father as invincible reasserted itself."

"It is remarkable," Molly said, "the strength some people can summon up."

"It's very little compared with the things David struggles with. I had to fight with our psychologists to hire him. I know he wouldn't be brutal, but he might be reckless. I try to arrange his duties to leave little room for that, but he knows I do and he resents it. Molly," he said, gently, "I have to go meet our man in Eirelief now."

"Where?"

"I can't say."

"Is it dangerous?"

"No, it's just standard procedure not to say."

"Honestly?"

"Of course. I don't do cloak-and-dagger things."

"Will you call me when you get back?"

"I don't want to wake you. It may be very late."

"Please."

"I'm not minimizing the danger. There isn't any and you could face it if there were. This meeting happens to be at night, but it might as well be a business lunch. Why don't you concentrate on the Moral Majority and pass the evening in righteous anger?"

She took his advice and decided it would be good to hear what Peter had to say about the contributors.

"What a pleasure it is to hear from you," Peter said when she called. "What a nice surprise. Tell me what I can do for you." His voice went mellifluously on. Nothing in the world like that *ex tempore* speech training. Peter Nolan had been, as a high school sophomore, a semifinalist, and, in his last two years at Cardinal Manning, twice national champion. One of his most celebrated orations had been taped by Molly's godmother, her aunt Rose, who had thought that, at last, she had come up with a boy bright enough for Molly. The speech had been a defense of some of the Vatican's more problematic political choices in the thirties and forties; and, at the phrase, delivered with an astonishing vocal range and perfect breathing, "Render unto Caesar"—pause—"the things that are" (with the *r* rolled) "Caesar's and unto"—pause—"God" (emphatic final *d*) "the things that are God's" (vowel longer than it needed to be), Molly had stalked from the room, white with rage, almost as incensed by her aunt's matchmaking as she was by the pope's collusion with the Nazis, and so determined to free herself from that shame that she could scarcely separate the issues.

Aunt Rose continued to champion Peter. He and her cousin Tim had gone to Notre Dame together. Peter's father was a custodian at a suburban parochial school, his family large, devout, and poor; and Molly's aunt and uncle had contrived, unobtrusively, to meet for both boys the expenses that Peter's scholarship did not cover. Whatever else one could say about Aunt Rose, Molly conceded, she was not a snob. Aunt Rose never missed an opportunity to say that Peter had not only a fine mind, but a good heart. "Brains," she had decreed ominously toward the end of one frightful Christmas dinner, "are not everything." Molly had never gone on a date with Peter Nolan and would not, for several years, visit her cousins unless Tim's sisters positively promised her Peter would not be there.

Now Peter had moved, as had the American Church, considerably to the left: liberation theology, draft counseling, migrant laborers, special needs, nuclear freeze, this and that. Peter and Dan Bloom had, it amused her to think, long ago crossed each other programmatically, both, as it were, epiphenomena, borne by different currents. The outrage Peter inspired in her had passed, too, replaced first by curiosity about his ideological evolution, then by mild fondness and growing respect for his competence. Political give-and-take had tempered Peter's precocious sanctimony; while Dan, rising in academe, had lost his dazzling irreverence and settled into unction. Moreover, Peter was moving heaven and earth, or at any rate shaking up the latter in hopes of moving the former, in the troubling matter of Timmy's annulment.

"First, Peter, I want to thank you. Mother says you've been wonderful about the family annulment."

"I'm doing what I can, but there are complications."

"What's the matter? Won't they take American Express?"

"Really, Molly. No, there are points of canon law involved. The new grounds are broader, much more compassionate."

"I'm sure they are."

"But they have not been exactly promulgated yet, and there's disagreement between the diocese in which they were married and the one in which they last lived together about how far one can anticipate in application."

"It does sound awkward. Everyone's most grateful to you for coping with it."

"Yes, I got a very kind letter from your aunt Rose. She's worried that Tim won't wait to remarry. And the strain is beginning to tell on Deirdre. She'd like to be married in the eyes of somebody, if only the State of New York."

"You should ask Aunt Rose to make a novena. I can personally attest that her prayers are always answered."

"She didn't do that, Molly," he said reproachfully. "She loves you."

"Pray that I'd be jilted? I don't suppose her special intention was couched in quite those terms."

"I am sure she still prays that you will be happy."

"Aunt Rose is conscientiously opposed to happiness. She casts about for pains to offer up."

"Molly," he remonstrated, "you have never sufficiently appreciated the eudaemonistic aspects of natural law theology, taking care to distinguish between pleasure and happiness."

"I have become careful to distinguish them, of course," she replied. "And, Peter, you do get more reasonable every time I talk with you; but right now I want to ask you about some unreasonable Christians. Can I check out some New Right names with you?"

"Fire away, darlin'," Peter said, immediately brisk. "What's it about? The murder?"

"Yes."

"Rumor had it there was national money going after that seat. O'Malley may not be spiffy but he is reliable. He hasn't cast a vote in twenty-five years that could hurt working people."

Molly read through the list of names, noting down Peter's knowledgeable glosses: "Nope, wouldn't be interested. He's going all out for some real madman in the mountain states; his staff wants him to diversify but he won't. . . . Maybe something there . . . He's finally grasped that all the bigots in this country are not Protestant fundamentalists; but he's not infinitely rich and he is principally intent on sabotaging black moderates. . . . Yes, and yes again, they are always interested in antifeminist women. No, it doesn't matter that she'd been on both sides of the ERA. They are concerned with textbooks, traditional roles therein. . . ."

"Soon," Molly sighed, "they'll be stamping aprons on female figures, the way they used to paint fig leaves on males. Would any of these people give cash? The records here are impeccable."

"Seed money, early on? It's a common practice."

"And a pittance to any of these characters would be a wad in Hooley Square."

" 'Fraid so. Are you going home for the Fourth of July?"

"No, I'm busy here. What," she hazarded, "do you know about Eirelief?"

"Oh, Molly," he groaned, "all our most shaming compatriots. The money comes from men who are the first in their family to join a country club and hanker to be back in a more congenial bar. The operatives come, as you'd expect, from the more congenial bars. They may not be essential to maintaining the violence in Ulster; but many of them are ugly and none of them is experienced. I tell you it's a miracle some poor cop hasn't been killed when he stops one of them for speeding and finds a van full of antiaircraft guns. You still there, Molly?"

"Yes," came the strangled reply.

"You aren't planning to tangle with them directly in this campaign, are you? I think they could be very dangerous."

"No, their only avowed sympathizer is no longer in the race."

"Okay. Take care, Molly," Peter said. "You should try to get more rest; you sound as if you're coming down with a cold."

(1 3)

DAVID DEBATED THE ISSUE with himself at length.
Nick had said he would stop back later that night, talk
the meeting over with him, and write up some notes for
the file. Nick made a point of doing that. Information,
even hunches that were beginning to be ramified and
potentially useful, should be put, as soon as they feasibly
could be, in a form intelligible to other people. It disciplined your own speculatious to write them down and,
under lots of circumstances, investigations might have to
be carried on by somebody else. David admired that in
him, that mixture of personal and impersonal. He played
hunches, he was often unorthodox; but—and it seemed
to be a principle, not just the way he was—he was not a
loner. He was the first person who had been able to con-
vey to David the value of institutions. David hated the

administrative side of police work, and said, peevishly, that he did not want to be a bureaucrat.

"David," Nick had said, "there are efficient bureaucracies and inefficient ones. They can be corrupt or honest, arbitrary or reasonable. But have you considered the alternative to orderly procedures?"

"I see a theme emerging," David conceded, "but Captain Murphy asked me again, today, if I wanted to go back to Northeastern. The department will pay for me to get my CPA."

"I hope you were civil," Nick cautioned. "Two of his sons are CPAs."

"Sure I was civil. I said I'd think it over."

So where was Nick? It was four in the morning. The meeting was supposed to be at eleven. It couldn't take five hours to hear about the supposed Eirelief-IRA summit in Portsmouth. The guy said there wasn't much to tell but that he'd rather not talk over the phone. Nick thought he was a little overcautious, self-important. But Nick downplayed the risks. At first David had thought it was part of Nick's attempt to take the glamour out of violence for him. Later he had come to see that Nick really didn't care about danger. It did not excite or attract or much preoccupy him. He dealt with it because it had to be dealt with. So where was he? Was he in trouble? This guy, who maybe wasn't their brightest contact, could have led him into something messy. The guys undercover in dope, now they were subtle. This guy was not subtle but he wasn't stupid, so you never knew how far off the mark he was.

It was 4:45. Nick must have finished with him early and, because his information was worthless, decided there was no need to write it up. Or it may have taken so long to get the story straight that he had decided to sleep first, and come in the next morning. He'd be sore if he called and woke him up. On the other hand, he said he'd check in. You were supposed to, if you said you were going to. David had neglected to do that once and caught hell for it from Nick. David decided to call him. How many rings? Ten, twelve, he's sound asleep. He wasn't there.

Oh, Levinson, you jerk, David thought. They must be sleeping together. That's where he is. She would be a good reason to go straight to bed rather than back to work. Still, he had said he'd come back. Nick had never failed to do that, except for the time he got a concussion. Could he call her house? No, that was too much. But Nick had positively said he would be back around 2:30. "It's unlikely," he had said, "they are connected with this at all; but we might as well know what they are planning. You're on duty tonight, aren't you? Then, I'll see you when I get in. I want to hear your reactions."

"You bet," he had answered. "Nobody in the department can match my expertise with ethnic vigilantes."

"We all rely on you, Dave," he had said. "I'll see you later."

Nick could be in trouble. How can I call this lady professor at 5:00 A.M. and ask her if she's having an affair with my boss?

"Professor Rafferty?" She answered after the first ring.

"Yes, who is this?"

"Professor, this is David Levinson."

"David, what's the matter? Has something happened

to Nick?" She sounded wide awake with the sort of controlled agony in her voice he had heard a few times in
women who did not break down.

"No, no, I thought he might be there. I'm trying to
find him."

"He left here hours ago," she said.

"I'm sorry to disturb you."

"It's perfectly all right." She did not seem angry. "He
didn't tell me where he was going. I wish I could help
you. He told me not to worry."

"Yes, he always does."

"What are you going to do?"

"I'm on duty tonight. I can't leave until I get someone
to replace me. I'll get someone to take my place and then
I'll look for him."

"David," she said seriously, "don't take unnecessary
risks."

"I won't. I'm—I'm really embarrassed about calling
you. I hope I haven't offended you."

"You haven't."

"I don't want you to think that I always know where
to find him or anything like that."

"David, it's really all right. I am grateful to you."

Nick turned up about twenty minutes later, just ahead
of David's replacement.

"It has not been an entirely worthless outing," he
began.

"Before you tell me about it," David said, determined
to get the worst over with, "I did something really
dumb. I'll do anything you want me to that you think
will help. She didn't seem to be as mad as she might have
been."

"Why don't you tell me what you did?"

"I thought something might have happened to you. You were a lot later than you said you'd be. I called Professor Rafferty to see if she knew where you were."

"When did you call her?"

"About five o'clock."

"And you asked, with your unfailing tact, if I was there, or if she knew where I might be."

"Both," he admitted manfully, "but she didn't sound angry. She sounded worried and real self-controlled."

"I'd better call her. No, you can stay, Dave. It won't take long." He dialed a number that was quickly answered. "Hello, no, nothing untoward. Sorry we worried you. Yes, of course, he thought it was the right thing to do. I'll tell him you interceded for him, shall I? Why isn't it funny? Let's go to Valenti's tonight. As early as I possibly can. Good night." He hung up and turned to David. "David," he said, "Molly is a generous-minded woman."

"She likes you a lot."

"I hope you're right. Now, listen, there was a meeting the night Mary Agnes was killed; but she had not been included in it."

"But," David pursued a thought, "if she'd gotten wind of it, she'd have gone like a shot any place anyone told her to go."

"That's what I thought too. And Ryan said she'd told him not to schedule anything that night."

"And Bill Foley told me when I saw him at Mulcahy's that while he was still working for her, she'd made a big issue about how he'd have to cancel any plans he'd made for that weekend and be ready to drive her someplace at a moment's notice."

"So either of them might have suspected something was on," Nick said.

"That's right. And the person who set up the hit might have counted on her willingness to rush out, knowing that she anticipated some call."

"Yes, Dave, but it could also have been coincidence. Anyone who knew her at all knew she was pretty indiscriminately enthusiastic. Will you go back to Mulcahy's and look into their mileage logs? See if any of the larger cars might have been to Canada and back recently."

"Sure. And while I'm in the suburbs, I'll finish checking out the foreign-car repair places."

David reported back later that morning. "A couple of Mulcahy's cars have made long trips in the past few weeks. And I found, at a place in Trafalgar, a badly damaged English car, black prewar Bentley, registered to one Edward Perkins, two addresses, apartment in Cambridge, farm in Vermont. He's an independently wealthy literary gentleman, lives modestly; the Bentley is his only extravagance. He brought it in Monday morning."

"Can he account for the damage?"

"Yes, he said he was driving back to Vermont late Saturday night. He'd been working in the rare books library at Harvard until it closed at five, had dinner with friends, and left Cambridge, he says, a little after eleven, and driving on a back road he hit a deer."

"I don't suppose he has the deer?"

"He claims that he has, or its burial site at any rate."

"Burial site?" Nick thought that sounded interesting.

"This is a wild story, not wild, really. He sounds like a nice guy. I talked with him on the phone after I checked the registration. The deer ran off after he struck it; but he was sure it was badly hurt so he went to the nearest house and asked to use a phone. A woman was there alone and wouldn't let him in at first. He said he didn't mind waiting outside so long as she would call the game warden herself. Eventually she asked him in and made him some coffee. When the game warden arrived, they searched the woods together. They found the deer at dawn, decided it couldn't be saved, and the warden destroyed it."

"What does the mechanic say?"

"That there was definitely fur in the grille."

"Okay, check out the game warden and the woman. I'll look into Perkins."

"I was wondering," Sal Valenti said as he greeted Nick and Molly, "if you'd like to have dinner on the roof?"

"Do you have tables on the roof now?" Nick asked.

"I put one up there. It's sort of an experiment. I thought I might make it into a roof garden. There's a nice view of the river."

There was a large table, set for two, with a low bowl of red and yellow roses; and set back against an outer wall, flanked by pots of geraniums and long flats of basil, marjoram, and thyme, a small wicker love seat. "Have a seat," Sal said, "I'll bring up some wine."

They paused to admire the sunset before they sat down. The sky was the color of the flowers, reflected in the river and in the city's glass towers, Boston luminous, prosperous, serene—at least as seen from the other shore. Nick kissed her and she began to tremble and could not stop.

"It's just a delayed reaction from last night," he said, kissing her again until she grew calm. "Better now?"

"Nick, I'm mortified to find myself so weak."

"Don't let it trouble you. There was nothing you needed to do, nothing you could do. But that must have been the worst of it for you."

Sal brought up two bottles of wine in a capacious ice bucket, and presently a parade of trays. He arranged their contents over the surface of what was a rather large table.

"Is it a family picnic table, covered with a cloth, do you think?" she asked as he disappeared again into a stairwell.

"I think he chose it so he wouldn't have to disturb us again for some time," Nick said.

"Will you tell me about last night? Can you?"

"Sure. The man I was meeting got nervous, canceled our first appointment, and insisted on rescheduling another, later last night, in an even more inaccessible and improbable place. That's what took so long. I was never, as I told you, in any danger; but I couldn't call you or David to tell you that. The news was interesting, if not necessarily germane. There was a meeting the night of the senator's death, but she wasn't invited. Evidently, it was quite a session: the Eirelief people whom your friend sums up very well, the Marxist-Leninist anti-imperialist IRA Provos who brought along two defrocked Dominicans as chaplains, delegates from the fringes of the White Power movement, and some others who had come to talk turkey about guns."

"Heteroclite."

"Very much so. Try some of this. It's very good."

"It's delicious. How did they all get on?"

"Well enough, apparently. United by love of gratuitous violence."

"Who were the others?"

"They were the obdurate traditionalists who excluded Mary Agnes. They refused to meet on that agenda in the presence of a woman."

"Dear me!" Molly said. "Libyans?"

"No, angel, they were gangsters and the only men there with any conception of a bottom line. They asked two questions: 'What do you expect to accomplish?' and 'How are you planning to pay for this?' "

"Did they get answers?"

"Not answers that encouraged them to prolong the conversation. They left within twenty minutes."

"Was Mulcahy there?"

"No, but he seems to have been expected. That's a little unclear. Let's go over to that love seat and talk of something else. You must be tired of this."

"I'm not actually. It's interesting. Oh, Nick." He had, in the days since the murder, treated her as one might an invalid wife. She wondered what he really felt for her. No man, she thought, could be more loving or less intent on love's right true end.

A pronounced footfall signaled the reappearance of a waiter, who cleared the table in seconds, left coffee and dessert, and descended again.

"I like to talk these things over with you," he said, "if you really aren't bored with them."

"No, as you said, it's most difficult when I can't do anything at all."

"There is something else entirely new. David has turned up a heavily damaged, previously very well-maintained black car."

"Does this one belong to Mulcahy too, or to the Bulgarians?"

"Neither. It's a black Bentley belonging to an Edward Perkins, who was at the Athenaeum, though not on the guest list, the night of the younger sister's death."

"Nick, I know him. He's the gentlest man alive, excepting possibly you in recent days. Was he hurt when his car crashed?"

"No, he's fine. He hit a deer," and he told her the rest of the story.

"That's entirely in character. He wouldn't let an animal suffer, and he'd inspire trust even in suspicious Vermonters."

"This is awkward, Molly. Do you know him well? Do you like him?"

"Yes, I do. You know much more about these things, of course. But this is a dead end. It's impossible."

"His excellent mechanic, the man who's serviced the car since he bought it, had the right front stripped of what he swears was fur and blood, and ready for the first coat of primer within half an hour of its entering the shop. None of his help caught a glimpse of the damage."

"That isn't suspicious. People who come in with Bentleys, even if they aren't of such angelic sweetness as Mr. Perkins, get pretty good service."

"Molly, you don't have to do class analysis to know that."

"Are you thinking he *planned* to encounter a deer, to cover damage inflicted earlier? Nick, he's incapable of hitting an animal deliberately, and how could he have counted on finding a deer, even if he had been willing to do it?"

"The deer may have been a fortunate coincidence, but he could have planned to collide with a tree or a stone wall anywhere along miles of empty road."

"And why do you suppose Ned Perkins would want to kill Mary Agnes? Nick, I don't see what you're getting at." But she did. "Maxwell's a lucky man," Ned had said that night at the Athenaeum, the night of the first murder. He himself, though she had been too unhappy to notice it, had been wistful then.

And she recalled the exquisite courtesy with which Nell had greeted him, and the way she had said good night to him, not kissing him as, indeed, the undemonstrative Warden had done, but giving him both her hands and saying she hoped they might see more of him now that they were in New England. Kill for her? That seemed a little drastic. Shield her? Very likely. But Nell would not kill.

"Perkins was a Rhodes Scholar," he said.

"And runs down IRA groupies with his Bentley out of nostalgia for Oxford? I think Boggle is a far likelier villain than Mr. Perkins."

"I said this is new information. I'm free-associating.

Apparently he was in one of the very first postwar classes."

Roughly contemporary with the Maxwells, she thought, with sickening wariness. "Nick, this cannot be. This is impossible."

"There's probably some simple technical way to exclude him. The particles of paint that were taken from the corpse may not match his car. I shouldn't have mentioned it at all."

$\left(14\right)$

IN DEATH AS IN LIFE, Mary Agnes's attainments dwarfed those of her sisters. The flowers eventually filled every Catholic hospital from Portland to Providence, but the most remarkable feature of her wake was the IRA honor guard, which announced its intention not to leave the side of their fallen sister until she was laid to rest. ("Probably plan to steal the body themselves and say she's risen," Margaret Donahue said.) News of their pledge reached Father Reynard and he spoke gently but firmly to Mr. O'Pake. "I know Mary Agnes believed in them, and in most things I would respect the wishes of the dead, but I cannot have men in the trappings of a terrorist organization in the church. The church is open to all, of course; they can come as worshipers or mourners—as scoffers if they behave themselves decently—but they can't come with their paraphernalia."

"Father," O'Pake proposed, "what about flags, will you let them in with flags?"

"Flags, I suppose so, the American flag, the Irish flag, the papal flag if they like, but no sidearms and no regalia, nothing military or paramilitary," he emphasized.

O'Pake conveyed this to the boys and they sent their crack theoretician to see Father Reynard. The priest received the envoy in the rectory, listened to him for three minutes, succinctly set forth Church doctrine on the legitimate uses of force, and asked his housekeeper to see the man out.

The IRA delegate attempted a more personal appeal. The priest replied that he had never regarded French Canada as part of the Third World, and that he would pray for him.

The honor guard decided, when they heard how the cleric had dealt with their comrade, that greatly as their presence next the bier might console the bereaved, they must reject O'Pake's ignoble compromise. They would wait, in uniform, outside the church and, on motor-cycles, accompany the hearse to the cemetery gate.

Father Reynard called Joe Calabrese. "Can't you stop them? Don't they need a parade permit?"

"It's not a parade, Father, it's a funeral procession. Wait, I remember something. I'll call you right back."

Half an hour later, Joe explained: "There were munic-ipal ordinances, from the Know-Nothing era, that did treat corteges as parades and regulated them, to protect the populace from papish spectacles, but this city never

147

had one. None of them would stand a court challenge today. Sorry, Father."

"Thank you for checking, Joe. We must take the bitter fruits of toleration with its sweets."

"It's better on the whole."

"Everything else is worse." After a few moments' reflection, the priest telephoned Sister Jude to ask her how Mrs. Moran was feeling.

"She is much calmer and bitterly regrets her outburst at Agatha's funeral. She has written you to apologize for that, hasn't she?"

"Yes, I was somewhat surprised that she wrote, rather than coming to talk to me about it."

"She is deeply ashamed," Sister Jude explained.

"Yes, that might be the reason. Will she attend Mary Agnes's funeral?" he asked. "And, do you think it wise?"

"She does want to go and I will be with her. I don't think there will be any unseemliness this time. I have hoped she would find comfort in it."

"I hope that she does," he said, sounding doubtful. "Fine. Use your own judgment."

Newnham was bracing itself for the obsequies. City workers were entitled to time off with pay to attend official funerals; but Joe Calabrese had to spend a wretched hour with the Department of Public Works explaining why, though the city could supply black armbands, it would not purchase green ones. Nick and Molly had the *bocce* court to themselves; everyone else in the city had gone to the wake.

"Has Ryan been taken into anyone's confidence about the funeral?" she asked.

"No, he's closing down the campaign. I gather he doesn't get on well with the boys."

"Do you think that explains his furtiveness? Has he been sneaking out to meet with Belfast-Mothers-for-Peace?"

"I've asked them and several similar organizations, of which there are a number. He hasn't. They did argue about the IRA, though. One of the secretaries in Mary Agnes's State House office heard a nasty exchange between Ryan and the senator last fall. She thought it was something about manhood, that he hadn't, couldn't, do anything, not like the real fighters. She screamed at him. He left without screaming back, but the woman said he was shaking when he left—and, after that, his attendance fell off."

"Real fighters! Real men! So she did think about it that way. Those thugs loomed large for her. I always thought there was a lot of fantasy in her politics."

"Well, it's pretty basic."

"Fundamental, right you are. Nick, do you think she goaded him so that he pretended actually to be the others, got her to meet him, and killed her to prove he could?"

"No, I don't. Like the cop says, this guy just ain't a killer. And it isn't that he lacks courage. He's intelligent, there's substance to him. He's not very sure of himself, but he's methodical. He is working on something, but I don't think it is concealing murder."

"I think they'd like to close," she said.

"I can't imagine why. It's only two."

*   *   *

"Won't you come in?" she asked, as she took out her keys. They stood, reluctant to say good night, at her front door. "I'll make coffee or something. I wish you'd stay."

"I'll stay for a while," he said, opening the door for her and following her into the kitchen. He watched her as she put the kettle on and shook some coffee beans into the grinder, quick, untired, a little tense—there was more energy in her, late at night, than could be well spent making and serving coffee. As the coffee dripped, she opened a tin of amorettini and arranged a few on a plate; and they sat across from each other at the kitchen table, quietly sipping coffee.

"Nick," she said, venturing on a topic they could discuss, "what about Mrs. Moran? She's capable, too, isn't she?"

"Yes, but is she capable of anything, as the saying goes? It crossed my mind that first evening, when you mentioned Clytemnestra, that she might have wanted to kill her shallow, incendiary sister. Her husband was already dead; it's not a perfect parallel, but his death adds to it, because most people think Moran couldn't take the way the O'Pakes behaved to him. And this afternoon I spent a long time with her. The scene at Agatha's funeral made her feelings about her sister plain. I wanted to get an impression of her and I had to clear up the gossip about Bill Foley and her daughter. She is every bit as reasonable as she is said to be. She had been angry with him, she said, for being dishonest with them; but no harm had been done. Foley turned up one day saying that Pop O'Pake had heard it was hard for Kitty to get to the skating club on public transportation and wanted

him to drive her. They were surprised and grateful and
he came punctually every morning at five forty-five for
several weeks. They were seen driving together early in
the morning, but Mrs. Moran didn't care what evil-
minded people might think. Bill asked Kitty out often
and she always found an excuse to say no. Mrs. Moran
said they had little in common because their backgrounds
were so different. Her very words, I swear." He relished
telling her that and she smiled at the pleasure it gave
him.

"What is his background?"

"Not the sort where children are made to do home-
work and practice the piano. He did not finish high
school. No one is certain he completed the eighth grade.
Still, the arrangement suited everyone and might have
gone on indefinitely—Dave says Foley's quite simple; I
imagine he was proud and happy just to drive her
around—until he asked her to go to an Irish music con-
cert, the sort where they pass the hat for Eirelief. When
she declined (she is the least intellectual of the girls, her
mother said, and the closest to their brother), he told her
it was her duty to go—Patrick would want her to. She
told him she'd rather get up at four and walk to the rink
than listen to such garbage. It was then that Mrs. Moran
called her father to cancel Billy and found he'd been
picking Kitty up on his own initiative. She was inclined
to forgive him, as was O'Pake when assured he hadn't
been fresh with Kitty, but Mary Agnes heard about it,
and was evidently beside herself."

"How did Mrs. Moran interpret that?"

"She said her sister always wanted to be the center
of attention."

"Clearly stated," Molly said, "without any Freudian baggage."

"Yes, she was more than frank about her sister. She said she felt no sorrow over her death. She had not heard of the accident for some hours after it happened because she was catering a private party that night."

"Did you verify that?"

"Yes, I spoke with her employer, who was positive that she had been there until two thirty and been driven home by her—that is, the hostess's—husband. She arrived home at three. Mrs. Moran's daughter Anne confirms that, as does her sister-in-law, the formidable nun, whom Anne had called because she was worried about her mother being so late."

"If she was worried about her mother, why didn't she call her? Didn't she know where she was working?"

"Yes, she did, and she called and there was no answer; but Mrs. Moran said that they weren't answering the phone and she had been told not to answer it herself because somebody was trying to reach them and the husband didn't want to take the call. They were going away somewhere the next day and anybody that mattered knew to reach them at the other number. Hostess confirms that too, though rather sheepishly, as does the phone company. Several person-to-person calls were placed to that number that night, from Washington, and none of them was answered. Mrs. Moran was indignant when she got home that Sister Jude had been disturbed and told Anne not to be so silly the next time."

"Has anything been heard from her son?" Molly asked.

"She claims to have had no word from her son. She

admits she is afraid he is dead, but says it's just a foreboding. And she holds her sister responsible. She told me she thought the woman, as she referred to Mary Agnes, was doubly deranged because she believed death for the Cause a grand thing and thought, tactically too, that a martyred nephew would be a real help on her way from the Massachusetts to the U.S. Senate. Mrs. Moran disagreed on both counts. She spoke about it coldly, as if she had looked into her sister's mind and disdained as much as loathed what she saw there. The primitive hatred she feels, that burst out at the funeral, coexists with analytical powers."

"Well, that's most interesting. Bess didn't think Mary Agnes would flirt with death, but I bet her sister knew her better. But Mrs. Moran couldn't have done it?"

"No, I don't see how. Though there is something suggestive in the recent Irish carnage. The army pathologists are still trying to identify the bodies, such as remain, of the men killed in the various episodes who were not British soldiers. They have some jaws, mostly with the bad teeth poor people have most places in the world, but one has state-of-the-art dentistry, and they didn't think it had been done in the U.K. Someone called me up to ask who was the best person to deal with at Tufts."

"Someone you knew?"

"Yes, in the army. The dental work was definitely done in Boston, but that does not entitle us to assume anything about Patrick Moran. You'll be pained, I expect, to know how many local boys do run off to fight in Ireland every year—or announce it as their destination to their horror-stricken families and admiring friends." He showed her a list.

"There cannot be this many. I had no idea."

"And those are only the ones we've been asked to help find. The sheer number is the reason my friend, the English pathologist, spoke to me first. He did not want, he said, to cause needless pain. He wanted to be assured that the matter would be put into the hands of people who would say nothing unless and until positive identification was made."

"That's the Brits," Molly said. "Hands dripping with gore."

"Are you going to the funeral?"

"No, I am not. I'm going for a long walk in the Scattergood woods. But oh, Nick, must you leave?"

"Yes, I think I should."

She clung to him when he bent to kiss her good night and then, resignedly, released him.

Molly went out to Scattergood with Nell Maxwell, who wanted, she said, to botanize in the college park. Nell made several classical allusions and, getting evasive replies, asked, "Whatever is the matter? That detective of yours is a man such as one seldom sees."

Molly thought it pointless to protest he was not hers, although his restraint perplexed and troubled her. "Have *you* seen him again?"

"Yes, dear," Nell said. "I rather thank there are so few clues for the second killing that he is reduced to going over the earlier one yet again."

"What did he ask you about?" Molly asked, as off-handedly as she could.

"Scheduling details, guest list, publicity—who might have known who was coming, whether we had made any special provision for parking. I asked him to stay for tea. Did you know he'd been at NATO Headquarters in Belgium? He and Alec had a chat about the Italian campaigns of the last war and how it was to be at Oxford afterwards. LaRochefoucauld was so right, '*L'air bourgeois se perd à l'armée; jamais à la cour.*' "

"Goodness, Nell, what makes you think he had a bourgeois air to begin with? I don't think he ever had one to lose."

"That's imposible. He's an American. He must have had, and there's nothing wrong with it. But his manner is better, more direct. And his diction is so pure. No euphemisms, no circumlocutions. That's rare in your country."

"Yes," Molly agreed uneasily. Was he direct?

"Are you seeing a lot of him?"

"Yes, quite a lot."

"You are happy, the two of you, aren't you?"

Molly said she did not want to follow that topic down to the river where the village women were doing their laundry.

In Newnham at that moment, Mary Agnes's cortege was making its solemn way through the city. At the principal intersections, hooded gunmen saluted the procession with salvos of blanks and then fell in behind the motorcyclists and trooped on to the cemetery. A skeleton, the banner across its chest identifying it as Eire, had been lashed with Union Jacks to the cross above the cemetery's main gate. Father Reynard refused to pass through the gate until the sacrilege was removed; there was a short delay while someone went to get a ladder and during that time a sound truck moved into position in a grove of pine trees close to the grave site. It played "Danny Boy" and "A Nation Once Again," not sacred songs but pleasing to the mourners, then a medley of dirges.

The priest, who had no objection to folk songs, began the service; but when the coffin was lowered into the open grave, the music stopped. In its place, Mary Agnes's voice cried out for blood and for guns to shed it with. It was a radio appeal on behalf of Eirelief that Mary Agnes had taped a few weeks earlier but not yet broadcast. A few of the bereaved had already heard it, most did not know it existed. In the pandemonium that followed, a man lit a cigarette with shaking hands. Instantly, an effigy of Margaret Thatcher, dressed with parodic accuracy, dropped from an overhanging tree, suspended by a rope down which some liquid dripped. The man with the cigarette tossed it into Mrs. Thatcher's silk gabardine bosom and ran for the sound truck. The liquid was kerosene: the figure blazed brilliantly, burning through the rope that held it, and toppled onto the casket. Earth was hastily thrown and then shoveled into the grave to extinguish the fire; and Mrs. Thatcher and Mary Agnes O'Pake lay at peace for a few moments, until the fireworks began and the sky to the west of the cemetery glowed orange and green.

"I heard," Molly said when Nick came to see her that evening, "that the boys outdid themselves."

"Father Reynard cannot believe they didn't break any laws. Joe Calabrese told me he calls up every five minutes with new ideas about ways to prosecute them. They did have a permit for the fireworks; somebody in

Walden city hall waived the waiting period and the site inspection. It was irregular but it was legal."

"Never until today did I see the least point in allowing the Church to direct the secular sword. I do see it now. What about the Eirelief appeal—how many copies had been made of the tape?"

"There were several versions, but Ryan thought they had all been destroyed. It was Ryan, by the way, who convinced her not to use it, told her she was the best known and most experienced candidate and it would detract from her statesmanlike image."

"The boys must have been outraged that she took his advice."

"I imagine they were. What do you think about the IRA angle, Molly?"

"She must have been more good to them alive than dead. Although today's manifestation suggests they feel a lot can be done with funerals, they couldn't have wanted to harm her, could they?"

"No, I don't think so. But keep talking, it's helpful."

"Is it possible that somehow she'd learned more than she should about something—and although they did not question her devotion, they thought her too dumb to be trusted, that she might give something away?"

"Possibly, but from what I've seen of them, I doubt if they would have reached that conclusion about her. They're not the *crème de la crème* of terrorists themselves. The Continental ones are, by and large, upperclass kids, reasonably well educated, not in technical subjects generally, but they can all read directions, which is more than one can confidently suppose about the IRA. The man in the tree who was responsible for dropping the effigy of Mrs. Thatcher was badly burned."

"They may not be good at what they do, but that doesn't mean they aren't always scheming. It may have been something factional. Mightn't one group have found a compelling reason, no very good reason, but enough for them, to rub her out?"

"Her father maintains that there was a double cross; not, he thinks, within the organization, but involving some Quislings up to and including members of the U.S. Senate. He would have tried to keep her at home if he'd known where she was going, but she would not have asked for a happier death. As for the ambush, what was McGonnigal doing there if those lily-livered diplomats who'd sell their own grandmothers hadn't sold out the Cause again? He thinks the functionaries of the Republic too eager to accommodate the Brits."

"McGonnigal was there, the Irish consul?"

"He did arrive at the scene promptly, considering it was almost two in the morning. He said he'd heard about it on the radio and thought it was his duty to come. He anticipated there would be a disturbance, he said, and hoped to help calm it. And he had a point. He got there no sooner than scores of others who came without any more notice than he had. Do you know him?"

"I've never met him. He's said to be very nice."

"Said by whom, Molly? The Maxwells?"

"Yes, funnily enough, just as Mr. O'Pake would have predicted."

"About them, Molly, isn't their son in Northern Ireland?"

You bastard! she thought. So that is what you have been wanting; that is why you cannot let a day go by without the pleasure of my company. It was a brutal, really a disintegrating shock. A bombshell—never had she felt the force of that expression before. Danny's marriage didn't compare, in megatonnage, with what was happening to her now. But before she threw him out, she would clear the Maxwells.

"Yes," she said, "their eldest, James. It was he whom you will perhaps recall being mentioned our first evening together as the friend's son who shared your admiration for Orwell's essay on Kipling. But you, no doubt, with your lightning brain, have already gathered that. Which branch of the army indeed?"

"Molly, any man who had been in the army would ask that. Don't you know anyone who's ever been a soldier?"

"My father was a soldier." He had volunteered, in the summer of 1940, lying about his age. It was a fact central to her identity, to the way she saw the world. "And so was Alec Maxwell; that he should be involved in this is utterly inconceivable. He is an experienced, judicious, disciplined man. He is not such a fool as to think he could protect his son by killing local pols; no more is he craven enough to kill them in that way. He has better means at his disposal to combat them; the day of the bombing in May he was in Washington meeting with fifty Irish-American officeholders, journalists, and bankers."

He put the question she dreaded. "And Mrs. Maxwell?"

"The female of the species? No," she replied, rising from the sofa where they had been sitting together. "No, she, although a mother and thus prone to dumb rages, could not kill anyone. I, though not a mother, could certainly kill you."

"Molly, what are you thinking? I'm aghast."

"Yes, I'm aghast too. You know that their son was not hurt last May?"

"They have already told me that themselves. Molly, sit down." She refused and he resumed, "Mrs. Maxwell knows or suspects something about these murders that she is concealing. I thought you could shed some light."

"Please, do not speak of light. I cannot bear it. But I will, gladly, tell you what I think of Nell. She is incapable of hatred. She would have preached against xenophobia during the blitz; she would have rowed soldiers back from Dunkirk urging them not to let their harrowing experience mar their appreciation of *Lieder*."

"That's nonsense." He stood to confront her. "Anyone who loves can hate. And if my psychology is primitive, your ethnography's worse. You are trying deliberately to mislead me with a picture of a dotty woman who does not and could not exist. Cultivated English people who share your enthusiasm for France and Italy invariably detest all things German. There are the others, the Anglo-Teutons who wish they could have fought alongside, instead of against, their racial brothers, but those aren't the sort who'd befriend you or whom you'd have anything to do with."

"How on earth do you know that?" She was so astonished that for a moment she forgot her rage.

"NATO."

"Then perhaps you know also about diplomatic immunity. You've been wasting your time. Now, get out."

"Molly, I don't think Mrs. Maxwell killed anyone. You're behaving so irrationally it makes me think you suspect her. I don't. I never have."

"But you thought she might just have mentioned something that could help you. And you'd do anything short of taking me to bed to find out. You do have scruples, or didn't you want to?"

"Not want to . . ." He reached out to hold her, to steady her; but she eluded his grasp. "Molly, this is madness. Think about the times we've been together."

"I am. But since it's you who've been releasing the evidence to me, I've no idea how your discoveries coincided with the progress of what I'd prefer not to call our relationship. No, don't touch me. Nick, I understand why you must solve murders. I respect it, I admire it, but I cannot forgive you."

"I want to kill the man who's made you so mistrustful. Molly, you know I love you. I know you love me. We have been . . ."

"As close as lovers? No, that we most certainly have not been and not because I did not wish it. How you could have tormented me, knowing, as you have said so candidly all along, full well what I did feel, I cannot begin to understand. You should have been less honorable, Nick, or a good deal more. I'd have preferred less honorable, much preferred it."

"I will not let you talk about either of us in this way. It's degrading. Go to sleep. I'll stop by to see you in the morning."

"I will not be here in the morning. If you have any more official questions, Mrs. Bradley, the History Department secretary, will know where to find me. And speaking of Mrs. Bradley reminds me. Just for a finale, for the last impression I shall ever give you about anything. What I like best about Nell Maxwell is that she does not use people. Everyone she deals with, acquaintances, subordinates, she encounters and thinks about as individuals. She's the sort of mistress who, without prying, used to know whether the people she employed were happy, and if they weren't why they weren't, and what she might do for them. I will never willingly see you again."

"You are overwrought. You do suspect her."

"No," Molly insisted. "No, I don't." Feeling incapable of further speech, she walked to the door and opened it wide. He followed her and stood behind her, hesitating for a moment, as he considered and rejected the thought that lovemaking was a simple remedy for her misery and his own. "You are wrong about this, completely wrong," he said, and left.

It was late but Molly thought she might call the Sternbergs.

(15)

SAM AND MIRANDA Sternberg had gone out of their
way to be nice to her from the moment Danny had introduced her to them. Sam, who taught labor law, had
been Dan's counselor when they were both teenagers at
a Yiddish Socialist summer camp. Miranda Boyden
Sternberg, an outspoken woman with the frank good
nature of one raised in great wealth in New England's
liberal air, had been particularly helpful in the ghastly
aftermath of the Bloom affair.

Molly thought that she would take refuge again with
the Sternbergs in their large, happy, tolerant summer
house on Martha's Vineyard.

"Molly, how lovely to hear from you. No, you didn't
wake me. Sam's away and I can never sleep. . . . What
have you been doing?"

"Nothing much," Molly said. "Everybody here is pre-occupied with the two O'Pake murders and it's getting me down."

"I should think Newnham's well rid of at least one of them," Miranda said. "Sorry to be callous, but she was about as bad as politicians come in Massachusetts. The crooks are less dangerous."

"No doubt about that," Molly said.

"Not that assassination ever solves very much . . ."

"Not that anything much ever gets solved," Molly replied.

"Depresing thought," Miranda said. "Listen, why don't you come down and stay with us for a while."

"Thank you. I'd really like to, Miranda. I was on the verge of asking if I could."

"You were silly, then, not just to say you were coming. We all love to see you and we have lots of room, you know that. Come tomorrow if you can. There's a ferry at ten forty-five." I wonder what it is, Miranda thought as she turned off the light. Dear God, can it be that toad Danny Bloom again?

Nick walked quickly away, oblivious to the direction he was taking, and found himself at the stairs that went down to the railway. The tracks led, eventually, to the river and crossed, by an old Boston and Maine green iron fretwork bridge, into the city. He decided to walk to his office. He passed the sheltered bench where he and Molly had waited out the storm. She had been lovely then, pliant and murmuring. And he trusted now in her good sense. She would sort this out and come back to him. But if she did not? If she wouldn't? He reached the bridge: the river narrowed here and flowed swiftly for a few hundred yards before it turned and opened into the harbor. The view from the bridge was very much like the one from the roof of Valenti's. Losing her would be agony.

He sat up reviewing his notes until morning, resolutely not telephoning Molly, though from time to time he badly wanted to. He looked up, haggard, when David came in at eight.

"The warden exhumed the deer's head and hide for me. He'd butchered it, he admitted, for venison; but he'd skinned it first and, judging by the coat, it must have bled considerably before it died. And there was a single bullet hole in the skull. The woman was equally convincing. She said she was alone a lot and men used all sorts of ruses to get into lonely farmhouses. Have you been here all night, Nick?"

"Since a little after midnight."

"Do you have a new lead?"

"No, that's why I'm going over what little we do have," he said.

Something wrong here, David thought.

"How was the funeral?"

"Inspiring. You'll be able to read all about it in the *Globe*. Their token working-class Irish columnist, who lives in Trafalgar, breezed by in his Mercedes. He'll tell us how in touch he is with all the real people who live real lives in Newnham. The funeral appalled most of the real people I know, but Sweeney will touch cultural depths I may have missed."

"Nick, you look tired."

"So do you. Tell me more about Vermont."

"The woman concluded by saying she was suspicious of strangers, but Perkins looked honest and seemed so upset about the deer that she didn't have the heart to make him wait outside. She made coffee for him and insisted he have a little whiskey. She told me again how much she disliked strangers and gave me some strawberry-rhubarb pie."

"You look honest too. What about the paint? I can't tell you how much I want to rule him out, definitively."

"That we cannot do, I'm sorry. The car has been repainted. Two years ago Perkins was visiting his sister in a place called Grosse Point, outside of Detroit. Should I know where that is?"

"Yes, you might as well," Nick replied.

"He let his nephew borrow the car. I guess it would impress his friends."

"I guess it would."

"Fortunately, he said, after the crash the car was in worse shape than any of the young people. His brother-in-law insisted that the repairs be done right there and the kid be made to pay for them. Perkins said he would have preferred to ship the car back here to the shop that usually serviced it; but it couldn't be driven a yard and his sister and her husband both felt his nephew should be taught a lesson, so the entire car was repainted in Detroit with a glossy black enamel that is used on several American luxury cars."

"And," Nick added, "although the glass would have to come from a lens that fit a particular car, we don't have any fragments from which we can identify brands and glass differs chemically less than paint. Dave, Mulcahy will be back on Monday. I'd like you to have a talk with him. Ostensibly, and, in fact, primarily, we need to find out more about his cars. He's been out of the country and ought to be able to tell us whom he leaves in charge. But I'd like your sense of him. He's garrulous, with strong opinions, political and other, he's burning to impart. Let him talk and tell me what you think."

"Is this part of my rehabilitation?"

"No, Dave," Nick said wearily. "It's a favor to me. I'd rather not see him. I caddied for Mulcahy one summer when I was in college. The money was good and he was very confidential and patronizing, told me what a smart young fellow I was and how many friends he was sure I must have in Newnham. All leading up to how, which he took for granted I'd know, the mob got its weapons."

"That's lousy," David said.

"I thought so, but I was a touchy kid."

"Like me?"

"Almost as bad. Get some rest and see Mulcahy on Monday."

"I will. Are you feeling all right?"

"Yes, thank you. Get right back to me after you see Mulcahy."

Nick called Molly. There was no answer. Then he called Scattergood College. The central switchboard rang History for five minutes; finally the college operator broke in and told him, in motherly tones, that departmental offices were seldom open on the weekend in the summer. Try again Monday morning. He thanked the woman and replaced the receiver. He wanted to talk to Molly. He wanted to know where she was; that he did not know even this filled him with desolation and panic.

He read the account of Mary Agnes O'Pake's funeral in the morning paper. Sweeney, writing with his customary condescension and bathos, did, as Nick had anticipated, affect to find a terrible beauty being born. He flung the paper aside. Molly, when she read the same column on the ferry crossing from Woods Hole to Vineyard Haven, tore it into tiny pieces and tossed it into the sea.

Molly boarded the ferry, spent by the past night's bitterness, and memories of earlier crossings crowded into her mind. She had gone first with Dan, the first trip they had taken together, a time of sweet triumph for them both. They had visited the Sternbergs often. Finally, she had gone alone; Sam had been away then too, and she had been glad he was not there. With Miranda she made no pretense of bravery, though she had tried to be just. Unlike Sam's, Dan's connections with Judaism were of the most attenuated sort. Perhaps, she reasoned, he felt that intermarriage would threaten what little Jewish identity he retained. She had offered this interpretation to Miranda, who dismissed it.

"You're overintellectualizing. And don't make excuses for him. He's not struggling to remain true to himself. He's a heel."

And as she generally was, Miranda had been right about that. Molly had been a great improvement socially over Dan's first wife—she charmed the kinds of people with whom Debbie Bloom was tongue-tied—but she could not compete with the second, who brought a political infrastructure as her dowry. No, Dan had not left her because he found her deracinating, but because the opportunity costs had become prohibitive. And what opportunities had she presented to Nick? She was too wretched to think of it.

The Sternbergs liked Molly very much and had made it plain they hoped Dan would marry her. When he did not, he became the subject of one of their rare quarrels.

"He is contemptible," Miranda insisted. "I wish Molly understood how contemptible."

"He's not marrying a penniless waif, that's true. Neither did I. I'm in no position to criticize him."

"Were you sleeping with someone else when you got engaged to me?"

"God, no. Sweetheart, when would I have had the time?"

"Don't change the subject, Sam."

"Dan is somewhat insecure. He's been that way since he was twelve."

"Insecure! He is a revolting opportunist and an incorrigible philanderer."

"Philanderer I concede. He's never had a decent relationship with a woman. He cared more for Molly than he ever did for anyone. I urged him, time and again, to tell his parents she was willing to convert and he was determined to marry her. They would have adjusted to the idea; but they weren't the real problem. He couldn't commit himself."

"And you regard that as unfortunate for *him*?"

"It is a problem for him. He's not happy."

"Molly isn't happy either. And what about the bride? What will she do when she finds out that he is screwing her father's receptionists and copy editors?"

"She won't find out. Molly didn't know about the others, and she's a lot smarter than what's-her-name."

"Others, plural? Sam, I won't have him in the house."

Miranda was there when the ferry docked. She was a thin, erect woman with beautiful hands and long ash-blond hair faintly threaded with gray. Her station wagon was full of tack and green garbage bags. "I thought we'd go to the dump on the way home. I meant to go before the boat came in, but I didn't have time."

Molly put her bag in the back. "Are you taking the latest issue of *Continuity* to the dump, or should I put it with the riding things?"

"Dump, definitely. They're doing their would-you-want-your-son-to-marry-Virginia-Woolf number again, and I won't have it in the house. I wouldn't, naturally, want Josh to marry someone like Virginia Woolf, but I wouldn't want Sarah to marry Malraux either, and I don't see that they ever write about *his* books in that vein. It's just not fair."

"No," Molly said, "it isn't fair."

"Oh, Molly, forgive me."

"Miranda, don't be an idiot. Who wrote it this time?"

"What's-her-name's sister. The benefactor's other daughter, the bright one who does things on her own, if writing for periodicals controlled by one's male relatives can be called one's own."

"Wasn't Dan involved with her too?"

"Everyone thinks so. I'm glad you've come. We're having rather a quiet time. Sam won't be back till next Thursday, but Hettie's here and you know how much she likes you."

"I like her too. She's wonderful."

Sam's mother was a creature of Social Democracy's rosiest dawn, prewar, pre–First World War, cosmopolitan; mordantly but militantly optimistic. Yes, Molly thought, Miranda had everything any woman could want; she even had Emma Goldman for a mother-in-law. Molly knew, of course, there were mothers-in-law and mothers-in-law. She had been cheered by the friendliness shown each other at the Athenaeum by the two Mrs. Putnams; and she had mentioned it to Miranda. The Putnams and the Boydens had been friends, it seemed, since the seventeenth century; probably they had gotten to know each other in Leyden, even before the *Mayflower* sailed, and they had remained close. Miranda told Molly that Hal's mother called Liz a godsend: before Hal met Liz he thought of absolutely nothing but sports. They had not known what he would ever do with himself; but since his providential marriage, he had become thoroughly public-spirited. Miranda's life seemed compounded of cheerful stories which she retold to buck people up. Molly wondered why Miranda had several times recently mentioned to her the Putnams' delight in Liz Hennessy.

Sarah Sternberg, a strong-minded twelve-year-old who, Molly thought, would make short work of Malraux or anybody else likely to cause her grief, met them at the front door.

"Mom, an awful woman came by, said her name was Mrs. Bloom and that she was having a surprise birthday party for her husband who really likes you and Dad and hasn't seen you for years. It's next month. If you can come, call her between nine and eleven some morning—

he works then and can't be disturbed and never, never answers the phone. God, Mom, she was a real—"

"Sarah, I have told you a hundred times not to use that word."

"What word? If you know what I'm going to say, you think so too. She is a JAP. A real JAP."

"Sarah, that is a very offensive expression. I simply cannot permit you to use it."

"Jeez, Mom, you say WASP."

"WASP isn't pejorative."

"Neither is JAP. It's an acronym."

"Sarah, that is enough. Go upstairs with Molly and see that she has towels."

"Sure, and then, Molly, will you play Scrabble with me? And, Mom, someone called about Tatiana."

At lunch, Miranda told her about Tatiana Alexievna, a Ukrainian general's daughter, married to a *refusenik;* finally they had let him go but had kept her, and a widening circle of people were trying to get her out.

"Sam calls her Tatiana Pogromolevna. But I ask him not to joke. The poor woman, I just think there but for the grace of God . . ."

"Go you? Scarcely." But, Molly reflected, it was like Miranda to see it that way and plunge in and do what she could. Molly thought it would be hard to find a situation that better illustrated the differences between the Yankees and the nativist thugs who had taken over the Russian Revolution. Suppose the Putnams or Miranda's family, the Boydens, really strenuously objected to their child's marrying someone like Sam, like, perhaps like Nick, or like her? At what would they stick? Damn short of locking someone up.

In the afternoon she played Scrabble with Sarah.

"Molly, oh please can't I use it? The *J* is on a triple letter, it's twenty-eight points."

"It's not in the dictionary, Sarah, and I heard your mother tell you not to."

"Have *you* ever met her?"

"Who?"

"Mrs. Bloom."

"Yes, she went to Scattergood."

"You don't like her, do you?"

"Sarah, I can't talk about former students. It isn't ethical."

"You talk about them if you like them. I heard you telling Mother about one from Texas. What did you mean about her parents' being a few million dollars and not more than five years away from burning the crosses themselves?"

"Sarah, do you want to continue this game or not?"

"Sure I do, Molly, please, please can I use it?"

"Yes, you may."

In the evening, Miranda read *The Wind in the Willows* to her little boy, Joshua; Sarah and Molly listened too, and Molly thought about Nick. She found that she could not think about it all, as it were, in sequence—she could not make a narrative, she could not state the case—she could not remember connectedly any series of events that helped her see what it was she needed to see. Had it really been only last night?

She dreamt confusedly and woke, at three, feeling miserable, remembering snatches. It was a historian's nightmare: she could piece together the several Internationals; failed revolution, yes, *rivoluzione mancata*, a change that wasn't really a change or not enough of a change; Russians directing terrorist attacks against Euro-communists, *The Red and the Black*, pink dresses, red shirts, Rome falling, heavens falling. *Fiat justitia.*

Miranda looked appraisingly at her at breakfast. "You don't look really rested yet. Why don't you nap on the beach this afternoon?"

(16)

"Hey, Nick," David said when he returned from Trafalgar, "you aren't going to believe this. I talked to Mulcahy and he went on and on about how good Israeli machine guns are."

"I knew you'd enjoy meeting him. Did he ask you where to get them wholesale?"

"Just about. He talks a lot. He told me he had friends all over and kept hinting that if I found small infractions, I should go easy, but he was happy to cooperate about the senator's death. He regrets it leaves Harrigan a clear field. He doesn't like his son-in-law."

"What did he say about Bill Foley?"

"I'm getting to that. Don't you want to hear what he said about Harrigan?"

"Not particularly. Is it relevant?"

"You always say anything might be relevant," David reminded him.

"Okay. Let's have Mulcahy's view of Harrigan," Nick said resignedly.

"He doesn't like him. He can't believe his daughter knows or cares so little about his carryings-on. Worse than that, in his eyes, you can't count on him for anything. You can't get a straight answer from him about whether he'd vote to keep out Jap cars or not and he won't do anything for Ireland."

"Did Mulcahy say anything about the Eirelief radio spot?"

"You told me to be cautious about that; but he brought it up himself. He thought it was stupid not to run it; in a primary, he said, you've got to get your own people to the polls. Excitement helps. Besides, he suspected that Harrigan had gotten hold of a copy and might release it himself, after editing it somehow, he said, to make her look bad. Mulcahy thought she should preempt Harrigan and go for it; but Senator O'Pake didn't trust him. She thought he was backing Harrigan because, whatever else he may be, he's still his son-in-law."

"She may have been right," Nick said.

"Maybe, but I think he sincerely preferred Senator O'Pake, though he's pretty crude about her interest in young men, which brings me to Billy Foley."

"Yes?"

"I did not have to ask Mulcahy about him. He pointed him out to me and said he hired him as soon as Mary

Agnes let him go. He'd had his eye on him for some time, thought he was a kid you could trust. Not too swift but loyal. 'Yeah, he drank some and fooled around. What guy with balls didn't? But he was straight enough with Kitty Moran.' Then he went into a tirade about women: what did they want? He never understood why his own daughter had married a prick like Harrigan."

"He never minced words." Nick recalled some things said to him during his summer as Mulcahy's caddy. "Still, it's a little strange to keep telling the police how much you dislike your son-in-law while they're investigating a murder."

"He said something bad about Harrigan at every opportunity."

"And he kept steering the conversation back to Harrigan?"

"Sort of."

"And away from Billy Foley?" Nick asked.

"No, he had a lot to say about Foley too. He said the O'Pakes didn't want somebody who wasn't a college kid hanging around the girl. And he offered another reason—he's pretty foul-mouthed—for why Mary Agnes was as mad as she seems to have been."

"Something about which Mrs. Moran concurs. Mary Agnes did not like her young men to have outside interests."

"Yes, you mentioned that. I think Foley must have told him everything Miss O'Pake said to him. He seemed well informed about the scene they had when she fired him."

"I can believe there's good rapport between them.

Mulcahy doesn't pretend to be anything he isn't; and Foley must have been glad to get it off his chest," Nick said.

"And about the weekend of the murder. Mulcahy said he left instructions for Billy to do a special little job. He needed a reliable man to drive some people up to Maine to fish. He implied that the men were well-known and more than fishing went on and that it would be embarrassing to them and painful to their families if the full story got out. He assured me that if Billy ever needed to establish an alibi, half a dozen important people could swear they had been together from noon on Friday until midnight Sunday. But some of their wives were suspicious already and he'd be grateful if I'd take his word."

"That's a better story than Ryan's, truer to type certainly—but Mulcahy has many friends who'd perjure themselves if he asked them to. It may be that while Mulcahy was supposed to be in Ireland, Billy was going to meet him in Canada and bring him down for the Eirelief meeting."

"He could have come through Maine without a passport in an American car," David agreed, "but he couldn't have landed anywhere in Canada coming from Ireland and not have had his passport stamped."

"That's right. I'm going to call Dublin. Would you start checking Toronto and Montreal and see if a man paid cash for a one-way ticket to any place in the British Isles the week after the murder? They are alert to that sort of thing because it's the hijacker pattern."

"Sure. But I don't think Mulcahy or Foley killed her. Foley could lose his temper, but I don't think he'd kill a woman in a premeditated way," David objected.

"He could have been made to believe it was necessary, his not to reason why."

"Yeah, I guess he is an 'orders are orders' type; it's funny because I feel sorry for him."

"So do I." Nick was uncharacteristically glum. Maybe professors didn't get involved with cops. But she had seemed as involved as anybody could get.

"I'll make these calls and be right back," David said.

Nick looked much happier when Dave returned. "Listen to this," he said. "Two days after the murder, on the Monday morning, Mulcahy turned up at the American Embassy in Dublin and said he'd lost his passport. I thought that might have happened, so I called them to check."

Dave was impressed.

"They kept an eye on him," Nick continued, "because of his interest in Irish affairs and they were suspicious. He told them his pocket had been picked over the weekend at a rural shrine his wife had insisted they visit. She wouldn't let him report it to the local constabulary because she was afraid it would tarnish the saint's reputation."

"Is that possible?"

"Perfectly. But they checked it out to the extent of ascertaining that he had already reported losing some several thousand dollars' worth of traveler's checks to a Dublin branch of Citicorp and put holds on all his credit cards, so a few days later they grudgingly issued him a new passport."

"He'd know enough, wouldn't he," David asked, "to anticipate they'd check and back up his story a little?"

"Yes, when he was starting out he was not above

handling stolen cars. He knows enough to cover himself."

"Aer Lingus in Toronto says that two or three people paid cash for tickets; I don't think any of them was Mulcahy, but I gave them a description and they are rechecking. He didn't, though, if he managed to get to North America, attend the meeting."

"No, it's murky," Nick acknowledged. "Maybe Billy didn't pick Mulcahy up because he was using the car to hit Mary Agnes. Or, if Billy did meet him some place, Mulcahy could have told him the session was so secret he'd drive alone the rest of the way—and taken off in the car and killed Mary Agnes himself. Has anything else surfaced about the other suspects?"

"Perkins did spend part of the afternoon with the British consul's wife. They had lunch together in a restaurant in Cambridge. The guy arrested loitering with intent at Scattergood hasn't said anything to the shrinks yet. I mean not one word. What does Molly think? Does she have any new ideas?"

"She's left town for a while."

"When will she be back?" He asked because Nick looked awful and he was concerned.

"I don't know," Nick said.

David felt a limit had been reached, so he continued, "Do you think Foley and Mulcahy suspect each other?"

"I think if either one did, he'd simply ask. No, Mulcahy would certainly ask; Foley wouldn't. He'd probably think of himself as expendable and take the rap without asking. If he's the sort you describe, and Mulcahy had been decent to him, that is a possibility."

The next day was a bad one. Nick was able to piece

together more than he wanted to know about Mrs. Maxwell's activities in the days before Mary Agnes's murder, and on the night itself. And then he got a telex from Dublin. Somebody had been caught trying to cash some of Mulcahy's traveler's checks, and his Visa card had been found in the poor box of a village church, the Holy Innocents, in County Clare.

Sam Sternberg came back to the Vineyard some days later, and everything was more rapturous than, if Molly hadn't known them, she would have believed any household could be. They disagreed, so far as she could see, only about whether or not they should cancel their subscription to *Continuity*. Hettie agreed with Miranda; Sam said one had to know what they were saying. "They are saying, let's pull the ladder up behind us," Miranda said. "It's disgusting."

"They're doing their damnedest for your Tatiana," Sam reminded her.

"That's true."

"So, how much courage does it take to hate the Russians?" Hettie said. "They're schmucks."

Molly excused herself early that night, and Miranda asked Sam what he thought was wrong with her.

"Is there something wrong with her? Why don't you come to bed?"

"She is very nearly hysterical. This afternoon we found her on the beach, weeping, just weeping over *Salammbô*."

"Who's Salammbô?"

"You remember, Sam, Flaubert's bad novel. The embarrassingly awful one about Carthage—somebody was telling us about it and left it here. About Hannibal's sister and a python."

"No one will ever make me believe Molly Rafferty is into snakes. Sacred groves, maybe; mistletoe, maybe. Not snakes. It's unlike you to deal in stereotypes, Miranda."

"Sam. Be serious." What was her mother's word for him, "irrepressible"? It used to nettle her terribly when her mother talked about Sam like a Tory dowager about the young Disraeli; but that was long ago and Miranda's personal politics had become more pragmatic. If people did the right thing, their reasons for doing it didn't much matter. "Sam, listen to me. Is our erstwhile friend Bloom being faithful to what's-her-name, Miss Neoconservative?"

"How should I know? Come on, Mandy, I've been away for two weeks."

"Stop it, darling—please listen. I've rarely seen anyone so unhappy, not since I was president of my dormitory."

"There must be limits to your noblesse oblige. I'll find out what I can in the morning."

In the morning, Miranda decided to ask Molly herself. "Sweetie, what's up?"

"I may have done someone a terrible injustice. On the other hand, he may be the worst person I ever met."

"That would take some doing."

"And he won't sleep with me."

"Then I know who it isn't. Are there impediments this time?"

"No, oddly enough, none at all. We are uncannily alike. He did say he wanted to marry me."

"And you?"

"Besotted. I don't know what to do."

"I think it's been too dull here for you. I've asked Winthrop to come down."

"Miranda, how could you?"

"He's my cousin and Sam's colleague, and he's helping me with Tatiana."

"I didn't know he did international things too."

"He's moving into the field. Extradition. Asylum. The home front's depressing."

"Yes," Molly said, "it is. Very."

"She hasn't been seeing Danny Bloom," Miranda told Sam, "but something's up. I practically had to lock her into her room to keep her here when she heard Winthrop was coming."

"He's never been a favorite of hers. Poor guy."

"She's entirely lacking in compassion for him. Today she said that there were more nerve endings in his suede patches than in his entire body."

"He's not her type."

"And then she began blathering about climate."

"Climate?"

"Yes, sunny, warm places and cold, dreary places. And people."

"Sounds like Montesquieu," Sam said.

"It sounded like invidious comparison to me. She said I should understand."

"Did you?"

"Not altogether. I just love you, Sam. I didn't classify you."

"Darling," he said, "surely you see that this is hopeless. Molly is chopping Winthrop up on some Procrustean bed of racial theories."

"She does have preconceived ideas. And she is a lot closer to Procrustes' bed than she is to Win's. She seemed a little more interested when I told her he was helping me with the exit visa."

Evidently Molly did find something interesting, because the next evening she chatted with Winthrop all through dinner and sat out on the lawn with him until mosquitoes began to outnumber fireflies and the new ratio drove them indoors. She bade him good night pleasantly and he sat for some time musing and tapping his fingers on the arm of a chair, in mounting agitation and good humor. He heard laughter in the kitchen and joined Sam and Miranda.

"Well?" his cousin asked.

"Molly wanted to know all about diplomatic immunity."

Sam groaned. Miranda silenced him with a glance and said, "She couldn't have asked anybody better to explain it to her."

Perhaps talking with Win had helped. She hadn't told him anything circumstantial but the very effort to speak hypothetically forced her to be dispassionate, and he was so straightforward himself. When Molly woke up the next morning she couldn't remember dreaming anything, but the problem was solved. Nick would not hurt her for the world. He was honest. Her experience encompassed men other than Dan Bloom. She knew Win, Sam, Peter Nolan, Alec Maxwell, her own father, men who did not hurt people; men who, insofar as they were able, restrained the ones who did.

And then, too, Molly had at last understood. It had come to her from the discarded issue of *Continuity* that, deeply as Dan Bloom had hurt her in abandoning universal brotherhood ("facile, optimistic syncretism," he called it now and again in the same publication), he had shocked her more cruelly by choosing, of two sisters, the prettier, more traditionally feminine one. Nick, stronger and more magnanimous, would choose differently. Things fell into place. The categories held. There was a heavy fog; she could not see the wild rosebushes right outside her bedroom window; but she knew she had been wrong about Nick. She could see that.

"Molly, good morning. Have some jungleflower honey with your toast. Win brought it."

"Where is Win?" Sam asked, looking up from the paper.

"Running."

"The weather's miserable," Sam said.

"Has a little rain ever stopped him before?" Miranda replied.

"When will he be back, Mummy?" Josh asked. "He promised me he'd help me with my Spitfire today."

"Eat your breakfast, dear. He'll be back soon, and he always keeps his promises," Miranda said meaningfully. "Molly, come into Edgartown with me. I've got some shopping to do."

When Molly went upstairs to get her slicker, Miranda told Sam, "I'm going to take her to the old bookstore. I'll get to work on her preconceived ideas. I'll buy her something exciting about New England, something up-lifting, about abolition—or whaling."

Miranda was still looking for something suitable when Molly exclaimed, "Oh, imagine!—they have Trevelyan's *Garibaldi*. I read it when I was a sophomore. Shall I read you the heartbreaking part, where Anita dies of fever in the marshes of the Romagna?"

"Molly, you are no longer a sophomore."

"I'm buying it for a friend."

When they got back, Josh, who had been watching for them, bolted out the front door.

"Mummy! Molly! Mummy, a detective called for Molly. Uncle Win talked to him."

Winthrop, who had been watching for them too, came out to help bring in the groceries.

"A man called Hannibal telephoned, Molly. He said he'd gotten this number from the History Department secretary at Scattergood."

"Yes, he's investigating the murder. I told you I was in the stacks of the Athenaeum when the first O'Pake death occurred."

"He identified himself as a detective. He wanted to talk with you. I told him you hadn't retained me but that I would advise you."

"What did he say?"

"He said he'd call back."

Molly was very quiet after speaking with Nick. She said she would like to go back that afternoon, if the ferry was running; but the storm got worse and the harbor was closed. About four, she went into the kitchen to make tea and found Winthrop sitting at the table. Josh had worked zealously on his model plane, hard enough to place it almost beyond salvaging by the most expert adult; Sam had taken him to the video games in Oak Bluffs to give Win time to do what he could.

"It looks as if Josh inflicted more damage on that plane than the Luftwaffe ever could have," Molly said.

"I've got it almost fixed," Win said. He looked up at her and, with fingers sticky from airplane glue, brushed his colorless hair out of his eyes. "I wish, I wish I had a real Spitfire, Molly, some thumping Manichean struggle—so that I could whack 'em and whack 'em and whack 'em like Mr. Toad of Toad Hall. I know you would like me better if I did."

And what, Molly thought, could she say to that?— Win, you are just the man you should be. I wish there were thousands like you. As an elite, yours is, arguably, the best in the world, and you are the best, the very best among them. And if I could have loved you for that I would have done it long ago. Instead she said, "I'm going to make some tea. Mine won't be grand, like Toad Hall, either, but would you like some? Can I help you with the Spitfire until the kettle boils?"

"Yes, please, Molly. Tea would be great." It was absurd that he should sound so grateful. She had never been kind to him. Two weeks to the day after Dan Bloom's engagement was announced in the *New York Times*, Winthrop Boyden had called Molly, whom he had met at the Sternbergs', and asked her to go sailing with him—with just a few friends, an informal jaunt, he had emphasized, they would be sailing with some other people. She had declined; and he had continued, as if he had not heard her, "I'll come for you at eleven on Saturday morning. The salt air will do you good." As her grief abated, he became less high-handed, but not less attentive. She accepted only about a quarter of his invitations.

She held the plane's fuselage steady as he reglued the landing gear and reinserted the propellers. Their fingers touched from time to time; but they remained riveted to their task until the plane was ready for Josh to complete. He would enjoy placing the identifying decals, the tricolor rondels of the RAF, by himself.

Win tidied the table, while Molly set out the tea things. Hail rattled like shot against the windowpanes; trees writhed, peonies splattered, only the dense thicket of dog rosebushes stood unmoved. "Stormy weather," he said. "You all right, Molly?"

"Yes." She became in his presence as taciturn as he was himself. "Lapsang?"

"Yes, thanks." He frowned and picked up the plane, blowing on the propellers and spinning the wheels to make sure they moved freely; then he set it down carefully. "Murder isn't preying on you unduly?"

"No." She filled his cup, stirred in a drop of milk, and handed it to him. She knew how he drank his tea; and that, he feared, was as intimate as they would ever be. "Is the man handling the case capable?"

"He seems to be. Tell me about your junket to Moscow. Miranda says you think you can get Tatiana out if you go yourself."

"It's a long shot, but it's worth a try." And he grew,

as he addressed himself disinterestedly to a political problem, voluble, worldly, and thoroughly engaging.

He took her to the ferry the next morning.

"I wish you'd let me go back with you. I don't know what this man Hannibal may think. Has he harassed you?"

"Win, if anyone violates my rights, you'll be the first to know."

"I only want to help you, Molly."

"I know that," she said. "I'm sorry. No, he hasn't badgered me. Nor does he suspect me of anything. Win, I was with him when the second murder was committed."

"With him? All right, you'd better board now, if you want to go. Promise me that you will call me if you need me. Need counsel," he amended scrupulously. He watched the boat out of sight and then went back to the Sternbergs' and asked when exactly Senator O'Pake had been killed.

"I don't know. Some time the second weekend in June."

Sarah Sternberg, who had been embroidering "No Nukes" on her grandmother's sunglass case, looked up from her needlework. "Between twelve thirty and one A.M. on the tenth of June. It was in the paper while you were away, Dad."

"Oh, shit," Win said.

(17)

MOLLY DROVE UP ROUTE 3 and into the city. It was full summer now, sultry and lush, and she marveled as she always did at the ailanthus trees with their stylized Henri Rousseau foliage bursting through and over chain-link fences. Newnham did seem a Sunday painter's notion of the jungle: its flowers were conventional in form—rose of Sharon, hollyhocks, morning glories, and squash blossoms—and raucous in color, like the gaudy melon flowers the Brownings condescended to in Italy. Jungleflower honey! Oh, Win!

Nick was waiting for her at Valenti's, sitting at a table in the back. He came forward to meet her. They both halted and faced each other, a few feet apart.

"How are you?" he asked.

"Fine. How are you?"

"Well, thanks. And thank you for coming." He seated her, without touching her, and resumed his chair opposite.

Sal Valenti, who had been looking on, tried not to watch what happened next.

"Is he the man?" Nick asked suddenly.

"Who?" Molly said, startled.

"The noted civil libertarian, Winthrop Boyden. Is he the man who hurt you—afraid you'd quote Marx at Myopia or let fall that your grandmother had been a seamstress?"

"He's not the least like that."

"When he answered the phone, I thought you must have decided he was a lesser evil." Nick spoke quietly. He had gotten over the savage anger he had felt when it first seemed to him that Molly had gone to stay with another man. "I recognize that whatever else a man like Boyden would or wouldn't do, he'd never ask you to incriminate your friends."

"Nick," Molly said, "I did not go to the Vineyard to be with Winthrop Boyden. I didn't expect to see him there. He's a cousin of the woman I was visiting." She spoke hurriedly. "And he's never hurt anyone that I've ever heard of, certainly not me."

"He explained to me, very civilly, that he and a millennium of Anglo-American law would look after you," Nick said, not ready to leave the topic of Winthrop Boyden.

"Nick," she reminded him, "you did not ask me back here to discuss my past adventures in the melting pot."

"No"—he smiled—"nor those yet to come. Are you busy tonight?"

"No," she said. "I thought you'd never ask. But, Nick, what about Nell?"

"As I said on the phone, several things, potentially very damaging to Mrs. Maxwell, have been established. I am virtually certain she did not murder or assist in murdering either O'Pake woman, but I scarcely know her and there's a lot I can't explain. You do believe I want your help in clearing her?"

Molly nodded.

"I told you I suspected there were things she wasn't telling me."

"I remember that," Molly said.

"I'll never forget it either. It hadn't occurred to me you'd attach much importance to it, because I hadn't myself; and Maxwell was, clearly, urging her to cooperate. But now she will say nothing at all—with a great show of courtesy and incomprehension—and he's become considerably more guarded."

Molly looked helplessly at Nick.

"No, I'm not suggesting that you question her yourself. Just let me tell you what I know. First, the cloth—you did know, didn't you—comes from a dress belonging to Mrs. Maxwell."

"I recognized it," she admitted, "but she'd been all over the Athenaeum for weeks, working on the exhibition; and she wasn't wearing it that night. How did you establish that it was hers?"

"As you may know, there are very few places in Boston that still do the kind of mending called invisible weaving. The best one is in Waban, and there it was," Nick said.

"But she wasn't wearing it when the bust fell."

"No, she wasn't. It was in the shop."

"Then it's irrelevant," she insisted.

"The bust, you'll recall, was pried off its pedestal."

"In stages? That would be risky, and ridiculous. The thing couldn't really be aimed, could it? You think some device was put in place to make it tumble down exactly the moment that one of the two look-alike O'Pake sisters was underneath it?"

"No, that's a little more than I think went on. But whoever caused the bust to fall when it finally did had, most likely, looked it over to make sure it could be done whenever that moment came."

"That sounds reasonable, but none of this sounds very damaging to Nell."

"It gets worse," he said bleakly. "And her manner has decidedly changed."

"Nick, she doesn't have to talk to you at all." Win had explained the aspects of immunity dealing with witnesses, as well as those suspected of crimes, in every detail. And he had told her a recent international convention, to which the United States was party, explicitly extended these privileges to diplomats' families.

"Of course she doesn't. But you can imagine that the British consulate wouldn't wish to appear lukewarm in the pursuit of justice here. Initially, as I said, Maxwell couldn't have been more helpful, but now he seems to hope that I'll solve it on my own. He won't obstruct, of course—but he's not eager to get involved in sorting it out."

"But why even think about the Maxwells? There were two hundred people at the Athenaeum, invited, that is, not counting the press, and people who had forgotten about the party and had just dropped in to read, and the caterers and custodians. And there's nothing to connect them with the hit-and-run. Is there?"

"I'm getting to that. Mrs. Maxwell was seen in Newnham twice during the week of Agatha's wake, the week before the second murder. A well-dressed middle-aged woman asking directions in an English accent."

"Not even the governor would let anybody go into court with evidence like that, zealous as he is."

"She stopped here. She spoke with Sal and his description of her convinced me."

Sal Valenti, hearing his name, came and asked with imperfectly mastered concern if they were hungry. They were not.

"She was probably looking for *mascarpone*," Molly said.

"She'd go to the North End."

"Phyllo dough, guava paste, anything. Nell isn't the sort of embassy wife who's afraid to leave the compound. She goes abroad in the bazaars."

"Does she cook?" Nick asked.

"Certainly. Sometimes anyway, for the two of them, or if it's a small party."

"Maybe she was looking for exotic groceries, but she wanted to know how to get to the corner of Locust and Channing."

"The O'Pakes' funeral home?"

"Yes, and the other time she asked a patrolman how to get to Creighton Street."

"Creighton Street?" Molly was puzzled. "What's sinister about Creighton Street?"

"Mrs. Moran lives there with her daughters," he said.

"So, Nell was planning to murder yet a third O'Pake sister and asked a policeman for directions? Nick, I'm beginning to think you really wanted to see me."

"It's nice when public and private interests coincide," he said. "But listen, Molly, Driscoll is conscious now. He confirms that Mary Agnes did receive a phone call the night she was killed, summoning her to what she thought was an IRA meeting. He caught her sneaking out and threatened to keep her at home by main force, but she told him she had trusted herself many times with the boys and that he was welcome to come. She knew he wouldn't rat."

"Sounds like *The Informer*," Molly said. "Mary Agnes must have been completely out of her mind. Did Driscoll get to see the boys or won't he say?"

"He saw nothing. They were hit before they reached the rendezvous."

"Is there more?" she asked weakly.

"Yes, a bunch of partying art students saw Mrs. Maxwell leave the consulate—through the back door and out the little alley behind the building. One could, of course, question what they were partying on, but five of them, separately, gave idiosyncratic but definite descriptions of Mrs. Maxwell."

"So it must be so."

"Well, she was certainly out on the night of the crime, and she was seen using a public telephone in an all-night drugstore at the foot of Beacon Hill. Her husband was away. She lunched with Perkins. Molly, *is* there something between Perkins and Mrs. Maxwell?"

"Adultery would be no less abhorrent to her than murder," Molly said with absolute conviction.

"That's what I thought myself, but there are other explanations. He might once have cared for her very much."

"Nick," Molly protested, "Nell would never confide something like that. If she had refused him, she would keep it a secret. She would feel she owed him at least that much kindness."

"That is, possibly, some consolation for decades of unassuageable longing."

Molly thought about unassuageable longing and cast her lot with Nick. "I do think that she was, most likely, the love of his life," she said so quietly that he had to lean forward to hear her. "But," she continued, "I don't believe either of them would knowingly injure another person. I think each would go to great lengths to protect the other if . . . if somehow a misimpression had been created. Nick, maybe they each think that the other did it."

He sensed that she trusted him and felt, rather than elation, a solemn peace. "That would explain a great deal," he said.

"Nick," she asked, "what do you want me to do?"

"To think."

"What about, cars? What was she driving?"

"Their own, a small red MG."

"Have you found any other promising black ones?"

"No, but I did follow up on your suggestion about all-night car washes. U-Wash-It is a chain, and aggressively well run. They want to establish patterns of use. So they empty all the machines every night and keep records. Only a few of theirs were used between eleven o'clock Saturday night and nine the next morning. There are a few smaller independent places for which we can determine nothing, but one of the more secluded, little-used U-Wash-Its had twelve quarters in a machine on Sunday morning."

"Three one-dollar cycles?"

"It could have been three separate users, or it could have been one very thorough and obsessed one. And," he added, "there was a pair of rubber gloves in the trash."

"Surgical gloves?" she asked.

"No, the kind for housework. Orange latex, size medium. They cost $1.79."

"I know."

"But you take small?"

"Yes, and so would Nell, but she doesn't have any. She likes to cook, but she leaves the washing up. It wouldn't be natural to do that if you didn't have to. Oh, I do wish you could be sure about the car."

"So do I. Either it's one we've already seen or it's been insinuated back into normal life or—this would support some more complicated and conspiratorial interpretation—driven out of state or into Canada. I'll be getting a batch of reports from Canadian border crossings later today." He looked at his watch.

"Okay, I'll go home and think," she said.

"Aren't you going back to the Vineyard?"

"No, I can think here."

"I'm glad you're back," he said. "I've missed you."

"I've missed you, too. Don't you have to get to work?" she asked.

"Not this minute. Let me tell you about our other leads." And he told her about the man who had been found lurking behind the rhododendrons at Scattergood.

He did not tell her about another which, mercifully, had led nowhere. He had heard something about one of the other candidates: Augusto Cunho was a former school-teacher, the first Portuguese on the City Council, whose daughter, Dolores, was his only child. Nick went to see him and, after a moment's anguished confusion, Cunho had said, "No, I didn't do it, and I'll tell you anything you want to know if you promise me, man to man, you'll keep quiet about this. Somebody called my daughter. It may not have been Mary Agnes, but it sounded like her. Anyway, someone called more than once. I didn't know anything about it until I heard what that woman said to my daughter. I was listening on the extension phone in our bedroom. I told my wife it was an obscene call and that we'd get an unlisted number. I told Dolores what I'd heard and she admitted it to me. She'd been afraid to tell her mother she'd had an abortion. I'm afraid to tell her myself. I don't think they should be able to do that to girls without telling their parents."

"But there's no knowing what a girl might do if she thought they would tell her parents," Nick had said.

"That's right. I thought of that. And he's not a bad kid. She probably will marry him some day, but not when she's sixteen. And Jesus, Nick, the thing was done. What's done is done." He repeated this, shaking his head. "What's done is done. I'm withdrawing, Nick."

"I don't think you need to withdraw. Nobody but Mary Agnes would use something like this."

"I'm not sure about Harrigan. Besides, I'm only forty-one. In two years, in six years, I'll still be a young man politically. Those years will make no difference to me,

nothing like the difference between sixteen and twenty-
two."

Nick shook his head as he recalled the man's sorrow.

"Something else?" Molly asked.

"No," he said quickly.

"What about Mr. O'Pake? Does he have any thoughts?
Thoughts can't be the word, if an eighty-year-old man
has two murdered daughters. What does he say?"

"Same as he's said all along. She was martyred. But he
isn't felled by it. He's still directing funerals."

Molly pondered this. O'Pake was of the old school,
not a grief therapist. He just gave, dollar for dollar, the
most sumptuous funerals in the city, and many did find
them consoling. They *were* deluxe: shiny black car after
shiny black car pulling away from the church. "Nick,"
she gasped. "A hearse! Funeral cars! They're black and
the O'Pakes have fleets of them."

"That's right," he agreed, "and they do their own
maintenance or much of it."

"And think, the audacity to steal one of the O'Pakes'
own hearses to run her down."

"I think it's a strange notion, but we haven't checked
their garages. I'll do it myself right now." They got up
from the table quickly, bade a subdued good-bye to Sal,
who accompanied them to the door, and found themselves on the sidewalk outside the restaurant, unable to
leave each other.

"Let's walk along the river for a few minutes," Nick
said. "We haven't been alone for a long time." The river
gleamed dully in the hot sun, ochre, acrid, an industrial
river with a power plant in the marshes on the opposite

bank. Neither of them spoke, both shocked, in retrospect, that they had come so close to parting.

"When did you decide to trust me?" he asked at last.

"Right before you called. I had just bought you a present, in expiation of my folly, but I hadn't begun to imagine how to approach you."

She took *Garibaldi's Defense of the Roman Republic* from her shoulder bag and gave it to him.

"You are very sweet, Molly. Meet me back at Valenti's for dinner, will you? Sal's been worried about us."

Mr. O'Pake snorted contemptuously when Nick asked him, but he told him to go and look. Damned fools. Two of his girls dead and the police wondered if one of his hearses had killed Mary Agnes. Fools, damned fools. He didn't know why he continued to pay taxes.

But careful examination revealed equally careful touch-ups on one of the hearses, the second best. And a check on the inventory of spare parts did indeed indicate that they were three headlamp lenses short. Pilferage? Unthinkable. O'Pake had known every man in his employ since he, the employee, was an altar boy.

"That does make it look like Ryan or Foley, doesn't it?" Molly asked at dinner that evening. "Ryan, especially. He must have had keys to everything. Thank you, Sal, the wine is delicious, but I can't drink any more of it."

"Yes," Nick said. "No thanks, Sal. I've had enough too. There is a lot of pressure to book Ryan, but his prints are on nothing in that garage."

"Isn't that in itself suspicious? Doesn't it indicate that

he took pains they were not? Candidates' confidants often drive for them. It's the most private way to confer."

"Yes, but Ryan didn't," Nick said. "She kept him in the office. Preferred someone more imposing at the wheel. Coachmen types like Foley, not clerks."

"I see. How many were there besides Foley?"

"Several. Most of them also work for her father and therefore own dark suits and black overcoats."

"And they're generally presentable?" Molly asked.

"More than presentable. They are the fresh-faced, stalwart, comforting-looking ones who help out at wakes and manage the parking at funerals."

"And apart from that, are any of them suspicious?"

"One of them was spending very freely over the Memorial Day weekend. He may have dipped into the petty cash. Ryan admitted to me that he was unable to keep track of everything that came in. He tried to discourage Mary Agnes from accepting cash, but she wouldn't listen to him, probably thought he was as squeamish about money as he was about terrorism."

"It must have been dreadful to work for her," Molly said.

"Ryan was ill-suited for it in a number of respects. He isn't naive; and he believes there's little in politics more important than patronage, or not reducible to it. But he does think it's stupid to break the law. Even if the courts don't get you, the press might."

"Did Ryan say that to you?"

"He did," Nick said, "and a good deal more. He was loyal to her, living; but her death seems to have released him. He talks about their differences now with a degree of assurance."

"Is he willing to discuss their differences about the IRA?"

"No, that's a suggestive exception."

"Things like that can go very deep. Political identity's so often all wrapped up with autonomy and manhood. But you can't see it as being Ryan, can you?"

"No, I really can't," he said. "But I shouldn't be too confident about my hunches."

Sal appeared with the dessert menu, recommended *zuppa inglese*, and almost instantly brought forth a sumptuous pudding. "There's a lot of amaretto in this *zuppa inglese*," Molly said.

"Sal thinks I need all the help he can give me," Nick explained.

"Is that why it's called English soup? Is it for warming up chilly women?"

"You haven't, have you, the faintest idea of the way men see you? Sal doesn't think you're cold. No one would. He's wondering how maladroit I could have been."

"Maladroit? You? Nick, you are irresistible," she said.

"I was a fool to rush you. Give me your hand, Molly, then I think Sal will let us have some coffee."

She reached out her hand to him. He took it and held it fast. Then his fingers relaxed and stroked her wrist.

"What next?" she asked.

"I'll try to be more patient," he said, "and we'll have to check everybody with access to the O'Pakes' garage, establish more alibis for more people, try somewhat harder to break or substantiate Foley's and Ryan's stories."

"Did you take fingerprints from Ned Perkins' steering

wheel?" Molly felt that a technical discussion was about all she was up for.

"Yes, we did. His, his mechanic's, the housekeeper and caretaker couple at his farm. None other. And no prints smudged or overlaid by a gloved hand. Perkins finds driving gloves an affectation."

"You do think the hearse killed her?" Molly asked.

"I'm sure of it, and we're close to technical certainty," he said.

"Then you're almost finished."

"That's excessively optimistic. Let's say good night to Sal. You've had a long day, and I have to go listen to the voice of the people in Hooley Square. See what the odds are between Ryan and Foley."

(18)

"HEARSED ON HER own petard, eh?" said Margaret Donahue. Molly looked somewhat askance. Margaret had been so depressed about additional firings at the high school that Molly had taken her to lunch at the Museum of Fine Arts.

"You're scandalized? And you understand most things. That woman deserved to die. Think of the wicked legislation she supported. Do you know they've just laid off three social workers too? The child-abuse hot line is only answered now during business hours, and damn soon it will be bankers' hours. Talk about the banality of evil. And that woman. God, I can just hear her nasty, prissy, sanctimonious voice. 'Why shouldn't little children pray to their Creator in our schools? Nothing denominational. Just an Our Father or a Hail Mary.'"

"That's an apocryphal story," Molly said. "Even she could never have said that."

"I heard her say it on at least four separate occasions."

"She really was the end," Molly said.

"Don't you believe that for a minute. There are hundreds waiting to take her place. Children die, more than one every year in Newnham, because we can't assess how pathological their parents are. No one has the time to distinguish between the exhausted, foul-tempered parents and the real killers. And she wanted to lay off the staff we do have in order to subsidize Mary, Queen of the May, processions. And a lot of the kids who do survive childhood can't read, and drink beer in the playgrounds until they are old enough to enlist, and O.D. after they've left the Marines, who were, for many of them, the only people they ever met who noticed if they didn't show up when they were supposed to."

"Margaret," Molly said, "you don't shock me. You put me to shame. I wish I could sustain that anger."

"It's a gift," Margaret said. "How's Nick? You two still hitting it off? I saw him a while back. He looked troubled, more than troubled, actually, he looked miserable."

"He's fine. He's very nice. And you were right about how much he liked Latin."

"Yeah. But not too much, right, not the first American pope? That would be one hell of a waste."

Yes, Molly thought, Margaret and Nell saw the same things, but there were marked differences of style. Nell had said, weeks before, when Molly repeated a clever pun, "I am glad he enjoys his learning, dear, and that you enjoy it too; but I do not think his virtues are of the cloistered sort."

Finding the car was, of course, better than not finding it and required a painstaking, ultimately fruitless investigation of the past lives and recent whereabouts of all O'Pake employees. Many worked themselves, or were related to people, often to many people, who had worked on Mary Agnes's campaign staff; nothing there made sense at all.

The free-spending driver suspected of pilfering petty cash turned out to have done well at the track. Joe's bride, Patty Calabrese, visiting her great-aunt in a nursing home partly owned by the O'Pakes, overheard a discussion about billing practices that aroused her suspicion and led, eventually, to some indictments, but none that helped explain the murders.

Scattergood provided another dead end. The young man caught lurking in the shrubbery had been hospitalized. He had no grudge against Mrs. Brewster; in fact, he had, and he seemed to be telling the truth, never heard of Mrs. Brewster. He recognized pictures of Senator O'Pake. He had been borderline most of his life, a high school dropout, occasionally violent, but his outbursts had never had the least political tinge. He worked in a record shop, and a girl browsing there had taken him up in a moment of condescension and as quickly dropped him. It was a long time before they got that much out of him, longer still before he would speak her name.

Mrs. Brewster was taken aback by the injustice of it

all. "But she wasn't one of ours; she didn't go to the college; she didn't even apply."

"Perhaps she looked as though she did, dear," Dr. Brewster said. "She may even have told him she did. She may be as mad as he."

Public opinion in Newnham split sharply between those who held that Foley, though his temper was savage enough to allow of his committing the crime, could not have repaired the car, unnoticed, so dexterously; and those who held that Ryan, though deep enough to plot murder, could not have carried it out. Nick judged both analyses correct and struggled for some other solution.

He worked almost uninterruptedly now. It was mid-August, and an arrest had to be made before the September primary. The murder of a front-runner cast suspicion broadly; and although the accusations remained unspoken, they were never absent from anyone's mind. Molly found she had more than enough time for her own work. Bess felt confident campaigning and relied on her less and less; Molly anticipated that she would finish everything she needed to finish before she left for Italy within a week of the primary. She called the Dutch couple who were subletting her house. They were in Aspen, adored the Rockies, they said, and did not need to get settled in Boston until October. He and some colleagues were teaching a joint seminar in philosophy of mind; and he was not expected to weigh into the course until Kant in late October. She was a painter and came and went as she pleased. Molly, who could not bear to leave, postponed her departure another two weeks.

*   *   *

Nick called one day in the early afternoon. "Molly, Ryan has told all," he said portentously.

"Confessed? Couldn't stand her taunts and did her in?"

"No, but he told me what he'd been doing so furtively. He'd been going to law school."

"Going to law school, on the sly?"

"At Suffolk, at night. And that weekend in Falmouth, he was holed up studying, cramming for his first year's exams. He was so afraid he'd fail; he's anxious, you know the sort, desperate to please, worried he won't make the grade. He was determined to say nothing to anyone until he passed."

"How did you get him to tell you?"

"I didn't do anything at all. The registrar mailed him his grades and he started telling everyone."

"But how could he have gone to Suffolk for a year and not been noticed? There are a dozen State House types in every class."

"No one was looking for him. You know what he looks like. You can't see him, and there was no need to use an assumed name. There are five Michael Ryans on the rolls; they keep track of them by middle initials. This year there were two Michael F. X. Ryans; our Michael's grades were sent first to Walden, or we'd have known last week."

"What about the scene about his manhood?"

"He did tell me about that, though it's still not easy for him to talk about. He had begun to tell Mary Agnes that although he would always do everything he could for her, he didn't want to be in what he called a subordinate position all his life. He was just getting up the courage to apply to law school, and she had always helped him, so he took her, and her alone, into his confidence, and, trying to explain what he felt, he used the expression 'to be his own man.' "

"Yes?"

"And she laughed at him."

"She laughed at him? Margaret always said she was mean; I thought she was probably loyal to her friends."

"It does show her in an ugly light; she said some cutting things—that he couldn't do anything on his own, and that it was lucky for him she could find a few things he could do. I don't think the inversion of their roles had ever even occurred to him before that. She was considerably older and you know how Mary Agnes was treated by other pols—she was one of the boys—no one thought of her as a woman or joked with her staff about taking orders from her. It just didn't happen. But that scene got to him in some basic way. It convinced him not to be a flunky for the rest of his life. He walked right over to Suffolk and applied. But he kept working for her; he's not reckless. He didn't want to look for a new job while he was studying. So, *cara*, I don't think I will get away from square one in time to see you tonight. I'm going to talk to that woman again."

"Which woman?"

"The Cambridge hostess Mrs. Moran was working for. Clytemnestra's alibi."

"Let me know if there's any news."

At eleven the next morning he called back. "It's coming together. I want to tell you about it."

"I want to hear about it. Are you at your office? Shall I pick you up?"

"I wish you would. Ask for me at the desk. I'll be right down."

"The lieutenant said a lady would be calling for him. I'll tell him you're here," an alert young officer said, and Nick emerged from an elevator minutes later. Taking her arm, he told the man at the desk he would call in late that afternoon.

"Do you want to drive?" she asked as they walked to the car.

"Yes," he said, "I'd like to get out of the city. Shall we go to the beach?"

"Yes, let's," she said, studying his face. "You've got it, haven't you?"

"I think so. How do you know?"

"You are elated to be right, but stricken by the essential justice of her motive."

"It was the only motive that made any sense. The Maxwells and Perkins are worldly people. They know evil exists and they've a fair notion, as you once said, of ways to combat it. Mulcahy and his bunch are farcical, but however taken they are with their own debased ideas of direct action, none of them would kill a woman loyal to the Cause."

"And she was that," Molly said.

"She was. Mrs. Moran holds her, quite correctly, I suppose, responsible for her son's death. She will not say when she learned of his death, but I am certain she has known of it for some time. The boy must have been as impulsive and as defenseless against her family as his father had been. Her sister had killed, first with her

snobbery and then with her fanaticism, both of her men.
Imagine the fury she must feel."

"And the shame. Men aren't supposed to be weak and
foolish," Molly added.

"Yes, that too."

"Nick, why don't you tell me how you figured it out?
You are pleased to be right and you should be."

He drove fast, passing other cars impatiently, and
turned sharply onto the dirt road to the beach. He kissed
her abruptly and came round to open her door.

The dune grass through which they walked had been
bleached a silvery green and shone almost white in the
sun; rose hips and beach plums had succeeded their blos-
soms; and a sea of purple loosestrife, symmetrical with
the Atlantic, reached from the dunes to the western
horizon.

"It's beautiful, fruition," Nick said. "Let's sit here
where we can see the marsh too." Then he began his
narrative. "The Cambridge hostess was impossibly vague.
She reminded me of my old girl friend Kathleen, very
certain about some things and completely uncaring about
all the rest. But when I explained to her carefully that I
needed to know, not only when Mrs. Moran had left,
which she definitely remembered had been at two
twenty-five—she had looked at the clock to see how
many hours Mrs. Moran had worked—but whether anyone could attest to the continuous presence of Mrs.
Moran in her house from the time she arrived to start
cooking in the early afternoon until two thirty the next
morning, she did recollect that, after most of the guests
had left around eleven, she and her husband had gone to

the late show some place with two other couples. And they had gone back to somebody else's house for a nightcap and gotten involved in a discussion of the film. She volunteered the information that her husband had been brilliant."

"How nice for her."

"Yes, it must be a great feeling. You should try it." He had not, until that moment, remotely alluded to the subject of marriage since she'd returned from the Vineyard. Molly caught her breath, giddy with relief; but Nick did not pause in his story.

"The upshot of our talk was this. She cannot vouch for Mrs. Moran between eleven and two fifteen. The house, she said, was immaculate when they got back. Mrs. Moran was still there, and, oh yes, the dishwasher was still running. She remembers thinking that Mrs. Moran probably had a lot more to do than she had realized. She was sorry to have kept her working so long. She had left Mrs. Moran cash and told her to call a cab when she finished, but because it was so late she asked her husband to drive Mrs. Moran home himself. She seemed young, in a big house like that. It opens up whole new vistas."

"It does," Molly said, seeing new vistas on every side. "Alps on Alps."

"Because, you know, the night of our misunderstanding, I was impressed by your saying that Mrs. Maxwell had old-fashioned ideas about servants, that she looked after her dependents. She would protect Mrs. Moran, wouldn't she?"

"I think she would. Even if Mrs. Moran's son had blown himself up trying to kill her own, Nell would regard the woman as innocent, as helpless in the face of it all as she felt herself."

They sat thinking about that, and Nick put his arm around her.

"Mrs. Moran's grief must have been almost unbearable," Molly said. She looked around at the swelling beach plums and the sprays of yellow barberries that would ripen from orange to red. "Plants are consoling, don't you think? Life follows death so effortlessly for them."

"Life comes irresistibly from any healthy thing," he said. "Molly?" He turned toward her and, standing, drew her to her feet. "It's time things were agreed between us." He would not compel her answer by so much as the pressure of his hand upon her arm, but stood attentive beside her. "Say you will marry me."

"Yes, of course I will," she answered.

"You may find me possessive," he said, and she felt that if he had not taken hold of her, joy would have shot her up off the sand until her head hit the hard enamel of the August sky.

"That is what I love most about you," she said when she had coherent thoughts again. "You are scrupulously considerate, but all your instincts are patriarchal."

"My impulses at this moment could not be more primal."

"We are promised to each other now, *promessi*, that's binding, isn't it? Conferring rights?"

"Rights, yes, certainly, and obligations. There is a pleasant-looking inn we've passed both times we've come here. I don't know if you noticed."

"I noticed it the first time we came," she confessed.

"I thought you had. There was never anything lacking in our affinities."

Later, in a moment of heady irrelevance, such as comes sometimes between intervals of physical abandon, Molly asked, "Who was this dim Cambridge hostess who employed Mrs. Moran?"

He told her the name and felt her response to it. "What is it? Are you laughing or crying? Do you know her?"

"I taught her. She went to Scattergood and married a man I knew."

"I see. I met him, too. I can't say I liked him."

"You are very different men."

"Was he brilliant?"

"*Summa minus.*" She shrugged and drew nearer to Nick.

"I don't know how I can prove it," he said as they breakfasted in their room.

"You'll think of something. You called David last night, didn't you? He'd have let you know if something came up."

"Yes, I told him yesterday morning before I saw you that Mrs. Moran's alibi didn't hold up," Nick said. "He's been staying close to Bill Foley, trying to prove or disprove Foley's story. The feeling in Newnham, which you may not have heard, avoiding bars as you so becomingly do, is that Foley would be hard to convict but might well be guilty. Neither of us thinks he is, though. I've talked with him, and David has got him exactly right. Foley's a kid torn between insurrection and fealty; he presents this or that authority, the cops or the collaborationist Establishment, to himself as the enemy, but viscerally he's loyal and extremely traditional."

"But he might have done it, if someone he trusted told him to. Proving that Mrs. Moran could have done it doesn't mean she *did*."

"No, but did I tell you about the teeth? That was, thus far, the saddest thing about this case, her dead son's beautiful teeth. He needed very elaborate procedures, the dentists said, and she had him in there every week for years. Anything her children needed she got for them, even if it meant endless trips on the subway and endless sitting in the waiting rooms of charitable institutions. They were always well cared for. She saw to that."

"Was it you who told her?" Molly asked.

"No, I wouldn't force a confession that way. Someone from Tufts went to see her, with Father Reynard, and the X-rays. The orthodontist told me that she received them with perfect serenity and said that their news only confirmed word others had already sent her. I'll have to confront her soon with my suspicions; I wish I had more than suspicions."

"Can you get fingerprints from the inside of rubber gloves?"

"You can in some cases. It depends on the kind of lining, but the ones at the car wash had been doused with lighter fluid and set afire, and the fingers melted together. You will stay a few more weeks, won't you? It would make a great difference to me to have you here."

"I'll stay as long as you want me to," she said. "The documents I'll be working on have been there for two hundred years; they can wait."

"I won't keep you as long as I'll want to. I know you

have lots to do this year, and it may be less convenient to travel later when our children are small."

"Sooner, I hope, rather than later," she said.

"I hope so, too." He lifted her from the window seat where she was finishing her coffee and carried her back to bed.

(19)

DAVID WAS WAITING for Nick in the carriage house
that Pop O'Pake had converted, fifty years before, to
accommodate his first hearses. The O'Pake property covered a city block in the heart of Newnham. He and Nick
had decided to go over the extensive garages and work-
shops themselves, trying to establish Mrs. Moran's presence, if not, positively, her guilt.

Nick was late. They had agreed to meet at noon, but
David felt no apprehension this time. The man on duty
yesterday morning had described the woman he'd left
with. David wondered if they'd get married. He went
carefully over the hearse that had been expertly touched
up and thought, at last, he had found something new.

David felt sure Foley was being honest with him. He
didn't seem up to duplicity; Billy had surprised him by

his willingness to confide in him. He had wanted Kitty Moran, but he was perfectly able to distinguish her dismissal of him from her aunt's. Foley did not even think Kitty's family had pressured her to drop him. He himself didn't think he was good enough for her, just hoped she might like him. You never knew. He was, on one level and that a deep one, heartsick that Kitty would not have him. But he went on, drinking, messing around, obliging Mr. Mulcahy and Mr. Mulcahy's friends, heartily enjoying Eirelief. He carted around the amplifiers for concerts and rallies. In June, he drove crates of spare tires stuffed with twenty- and fifty-dollar bills across the Canadian border, and once he had sailed to Charlottetown on Prince Edward Island to help with the transshipment of arms. David had not known about either of these trips, but he had inferred that something like them had taken place. He knew, or thought he knew, the limits of Foley's criminality.

"That's right," Nick had said when they had discussed it the previous day. "Puerile but not cowardly."

Foley thought that Mary Agnes had been unfair to him; but he did not think she had forfeited, thereby, the right to command him. He was that humble. David marveled at his resignation and cursed it and he wondered if Nick were right, that Foley would take the rap if someone who had been good to him wanted him to, or if he thought that person did. David made a point of dropping in most evenings at the Limerick Bar in Hooley Square. Ryan's alibi, his reticence, and then his loquacity upon passing made perfect sense at the Limerick. Everyone accepted it instantly, and suspicion had begun to focus on Foley.

When Nick arrived, looking hastily shaved and more pleased with life in general than the case could have given him grounds to be, David showed him some scratches, like those made by a crowbar, around the rear door of the hearse. "I didn't notice them last time," Nick said. "I was concentrating on the front end damage."

"What do you suppose was in the back?" David asked.

"I wish I knew, but I feel it's idle curiosity. The repairs in the front were done deftly. Anyone who could have done them could have covered up these scratches in minutes."

"Maybe his work was interrupted," David suggested.

"That's possible," Nick conceded. "I think we'd better go over everything again."

Nick had gotten Mrs. Moran's fingerprints from the exclusive catering firm for which she worked. Their employees, the manager said, had often to be entrusted with priceless family silver, and as security for their clients, all were fingerprinted. But her prints were nowhere in evidence. Each hearse had, in its glove compartment, several pairs of gloves, black kid and black pigskin. No one entering any of O'Pake's cars, who thought to look, need ever put a hand on the wheel. Foley, who drove without gloves unless instructed to wear them ("I hate them. They're like rubbers. You can't feel anything. It ain't natural," he had said, and Nick had thought about high school and Saint Thomas Aquinas), had left prints everywhere, including on the crowbar.

"There's nothing here to implicate Mrs. Moran," Nick said finally. "And I wonder how she could have gotten here from that house in Cambridge, to Southie and back, and then returned in time to clean up after a large party. You checked the cab companies, didn't you?"

"Yes, and she didn't call any cab that keeps records. Of course, it could have been a gypsy, or an obliging friend, maybe an obliging friend of her son's," Dave said.

"And she is energetic," Nick continued. "It couldn't have taken her more than twenty minutes to walk from the Blooms' house to Harvard Square. Buses run late to Hooley Square, every hour around the half hour, I think. Let's see who had that run the night of the murder."

"But how could she have gotten back?" David asked. "Do you think she drove back in the hearse?"

"It's hard to believe she could have parked a hearse inconspicuously off Brattle Street. And Bloom, the host, says he drove her home. I don't know. Why don't you check the bus drivers and I'll see about places one might leave a hearse and return for it before dawn. Oh, and Dave, Molly and I would like you to have dinner with us tonight at her house. We can compare notes then."

Nick was describing the puzzle to Molly when David arrived with a bottle of champagne.

"David," Molly said, "how sweet. Why so festive?"

"I'm a detective," he said. "And I know what you're going to tell me tonight."

"You're right," she said.

"Nick taught me everything I know."

"What did you find out?" Nick asked after the celebration had somewhat abated.

"The bus driver said he remembered the night clearly because he wasn't supposed to be working, doesn't usually work on the weekends, but he was substituting for someone who was called away suddenly. Do you suppose there's some tie-in between the trolleymen's union and Eirelief?"

"Anything's possible," Nick said.

"Anyway, this guy remembered that and also that when he got home the murder was on television. It would have had to have been the eleven forty run; she couldn't have made it earlier, and twelve forty, which is the last, is too late. He recollects only two women, an enormous bag lady and one painfully thin girl, shabby, he said, but it sounds like she could have been wearing thrift shop clothes. Neither is at all like Mrs. Moran's shape or style."

"Can Mrs. Moran ride a bicycle?" Molly emerged from the kitchen where she had been absorbed in a garlic mayonnaise and told them dinner was ready.

"I haven't any idea," Nick said. "It's a good thought."

"It's a perfect distance for a bike," she continued. "An overlong and time-consuming walk, but no need for a car. I imagine the Blooms have bikes. Ruthie Bloom, as I remember her from Scattergood, always biked into the village."

"Do you know Mrs. Moran's ex-alibi?" David asked.

"Yes," Molly said. "It's a small world. But would Mrs. Moran know how? How old is she, Nick?"

"Early forties," Nick said. "She married young. She was the next oldest to Mary Agnes, but there were two stillborn sons between them."

"A girl growing up in Newnham in the late forties, early fifties, might well have biked, don't you think, Nick? And she is Irish."

"That should make her a full generation more liberated," he said.

"In the aggregate, it would," she persisted, "wouldn't it?"

"I suppose so. I love you just the way you are."

David listened to this exchange with amusement and added, "And, if she burned her kitchen gloves at the car wash and wore chauffeur's gloves in the hearse, she might have been barehanded riding back."

"That's right, Dave. Let's have someone check that out right away. Excuse me, Molly." Nick went to the telephone and gave some instructions. When he returned to the table, he said, "I'd like to clear Foley. I talked with him this afternoon about the scratches we found. He denied knowledge at first, but with a sort of hunted look. Eventually he said he'd taken the hearse out without a full set of keys and had a flat, had to force the door to get at the tools. I asked him how he had managed to find a crowbar and not a jack, and he said he'd borrowed one. He is terrified about something. You'd think he'd be spoiling for a fight, but he seems merely frightened and confused."

"Who's tailing him tonight?" David asked.

"Morris and Carlucci," Nick said. "Don't worry. They're both competent."

"Competent, yes." David was not satisfied. "Neither of them is local."

"Local?" Nick asked.

"I mean, they're from Boston, and they don't know Newnham well. They haven't spent a lot of time here. After dinner, I think I'll go down to the Limerick, where Foley hangs out. Is that all right with you?"

"David, " Molly asked, "where is the Limerick?"

"In Hooley Square, between the Teamsters' local and the Little Sisters of the Poor."

"That sums up Foley," Nick added.

"Nick," Molly said, "perhaps you'd like to go too?"

"No," Dave interrupted. "I don't need to go myself. I'd just like to."

"Will he be all right?" Molly asked after he left.

"I think so. And it's something he wants to do alone. Come home with me, darling. I ought to be reachable all night. I've asked the people working on Ruth Bloom's bicycle to call me whenever they finish with it. It won't be conclusive, of course, because Mrs. Moran may have handled—or I suppose even ridden it—in various innocent ways, but I'd like some confirmation."

"Would it be better if you went into Boston and waited for the results?" she asked, reluctantly aware of other claims upon his time.

"No, I wouldn't arrest Mrs. Moran in the middle of the night for riding her employer's bicycle. I'd like to be sure she did, but I have other plans for tonight."

Molly did not hear the phone ring; she stirred as Nick's arm tightened around her and woke to hear him ask, "What about David? Are you sure *he's* all right? Yes. Do that. No, I'll do it. Which hospital?"

"What happened?"

"Foley slipped away from the men who were supposed to be watching him. David picked up his trail, but did not get to the bridge in time to see whether he fell or was pushed off it. You know the Boston and Maine bridge over the river, just before the expressway. David went in after him and hauled him out. David is fine but he's being kept under observation. Foley's comatose. The doctors say the alcohol alone might kill him, but they think it won't."

"Did somebody get him that drunk?"

"I don't know. He certainly knew how to do it himself. Can you go back to sleep? I've got to get to the hospital after I call David's mother."

"Can she leave her husband? Does she drive? Why don't you ask her if she needs any help," Molly said. "You'll have your hands full with Foley."

Early the next morning, after Nick had spoken with David and seen Foley, he decided that the simplest way to find out about the perplexing scratches would be to ask Mr. O'Pake what he thought himself.

O'Pake maintained that he had never noticed them before; he left the cars to the younger fellows. But that afternoon he paid a visit to Bill Foley, who lay bandaged and subdued, recovering from his fall. O'Pake told the officer guarding Foley that he wanted to speak privately with the patient. The man replied that his orders were to leave no one alone with Foley.

"Have you charged him with anything yet?" O'Pake asked sharply. He was not pugnacious but he was quick.

"No, sir, but his fall may have been an accident, or it may have been attempted murder. We aren't taking any chances."

"You think he killed my girls, too, don't you? You're id-y-its, idjits," he repeated, his anger compressing three syllables into two. He turned in disgust from the officer, himself aging and weary, no hot shot or he would not be assigned work like this after twenty years on the force. "I'm sorry, Mr. O'Pake," he said, "I always voted for her. So did my wife. We'd have voted for her again. My two oldest kids are registered too."

"That so? What's your name?"

"Halloran, Jim Halloran."

"Thank you, Jim. I'll remember you. I want to talk quietly with Billy. Do you mind that? Do you want to search me first?"

"No, sir," Halloran replied, scandalized by the suggestion. "Go right ahead. I'll just stand over by the door. I won't be able to hear what you say but I'll be watching him like I'm supposed to."

"Billy," O'Pake said softly to the drowsy boy, "Billy, Officer Halloran here says he's got to stay in the room. They're lookin' after you. And you look tired, so I won't stay long. Are they feedin' you all right? Do you want a drink?"

"Can't," he replied, dully miserable.

"You can have eggnog, can't you?"

"I doan know. I like it straight."

"You'll like it in eggnog, if that's all they'll let you have," he said *sotto voce.* "Nurse!" he bellowed; and when the eggnog was brought, he doused it generously from a flask in his breast pocket. "Billy," he said gravely, drawing closer to him, "tell the police the truth about the money. Be honest, and I'll see that no harm comes to you. Nobody's going to care about a little thing like that. You don't know who killed them, do you?"

Billy shook his head sadly at the question, but he seemed to take heart.

"What did you do with the money you took from the

hearse?" O'Pake pursued, more softly still. "Did you go on a spree?"

Foley, horrified, shook his head again, violently this time, and began to cough. The spasm subsided and he gasped out, "No, no, I didn't spend it. I didn't steal it. I took it and gave it to Mr. Mulcahy."

"I understand. She'd have wanted it to go to them," he continued in a whisper. "I'll tell the police I told you to . . . but to make it look like a heist, in case anybody unreliable asked about it. But don't tell them that yourself. They'll respect us both more if each of us takes responsibility. You understand that, don't you?"

Billy nodded.

"You're a good boy, Billy. I'll tell Kitty, too."

"Don't, Pop, don't bother." Billy spoke from a great depth of sorrow. "It won't make no difference to her."

"Maybe it won't, but she should know what really happened."

O'Pake called Mulcahy and verified that Billy had given Eirelief the cash Mary Agnes had illegally accepted for her campaign. Mary Agnes had kept the money in a strongbox hidden with the tool kit in the back of a hearse. "The police found the scratches," O'Pake said, "and his prints on the crowbar he forced it with. I'm going to tell them I told him to do it. The police are fools."

"Hannibal's not a fool," Mulcahy said. "I knew him when he was a kid. And he's clean. But he doesn't know what happened to Billy. I don't know myself. Some of the boys wanted to kill him. Others think he's innocent. And then there's a crowd of them want a trial, to educate public opinion," Mulcahy confided.

"Holy Mother of God," O'Pake exploded. "They want that boy to stand trial for murder to educate public opinion?"

"Yeah," Mulcahy said. "I told them it was a dumb idea."

"How's your son-in-law doing?" O'Pake changed the subject tactfully.

"Oh, Jesus, he's worse than any of them." The new topic was not one that cheered Mulcahy, and he held forth, with many racy particulars, on his son-in-law's failings.

O'Pake listened sympathetically and concluded: "I'll tell Hannibal about the money. But I'll tell him Billy gave it directly to an Irish national in Canada."

He did, and then he went to see his daughter, Mrs. Moran. She lived in the middle flat of a triple-decker in one of Newnham's drearier wards. He labored up the stairs to her apartment; the floors and the cheap pine wainscoting, like the linoleum in the kitchen, were worn from much scrubbing. His daughter, who had fought the struggle for propriety, was not exhausted by it. She listened to her father's story and then asked quietly, "Do you think they tried to kill him? Will they try again?"

"I don't know what really happened, but there's a guard in his room. He's safe."

"The police can't guard him forever," she said grimly. "Pop, I have to go to work now. I'm late already."

"I'll take you," he said. "Where do you have to go?"

"I'll take the subway," she said. "Thank you, I'll go by myself."

They were not a demonstrative family. Her father had not struck her when she told him that she had to marry Patrick, but they had not touched each other in affection since that day either. Now she kissed her father good-bye and he bent stiffly and kissed her forehead.

"You were not a bad girl, Maddy," he said.

"No, Pop, I was not," she answered. "Now, you must excuse me. I must get ready." She walked her father down to the curb and then went back upstairs to change her clothes. She dressed quickly, in a gray linen dress with a jacket that one of her ladies had given her. It was, of all her clothes, the most businesslike. Her doorbell rang and she hurried to answer it, impatient to be on her way.

"Lieutenant Hannibal?" she said. "I was coming to see you."

"Mrs. Moran," Nick began, pausing at the threshold. It was evident she was dressed for an errand she took seriously. She stood before him, full-bosomed, short-limbed, her broad strong hands in white cotton gloves, her ample body solid, not slack. Ladylike. She should have presided over a happy house, dispensing plenty.

"Come in, Lieutenant," she said. "Please sit down. I was coming to tell you that I killed my sisters. I did not think you knew that I did, and my father told me Bill Foley is suspected. An attempt was made on his life, or perhaps he was so frightened and friendless that, in a stupor, he nearly killed himself."

"Mrs. Moran," he interrupted, "let me tell you your rights."

"I know my rights," she replied composedly.

"Nevertheless, I must formally read them to you. Please let me do that." When he had finished, he said, "I had come to ask you under what circumstances you rode Mrs. Bloom's bicycle."

"You were clever to think of that," she said.

"It was clever. But I wasn't the one who thought of it," he said.

Mrs. Moran then readily explained that she believed her sister would, as long as she lived, wreak havoc. She had not turned herself in because two of her children were not yet self-supporting and she did not wish her family to be a burden to anyone. They, the clan or extended family, were responsible for enough suffering as it was. She had left work shortly after the Blooms went out, having telephoned her sister during the party, which had provided an amount of background noise, to set up a rendezvous, supposedly with the Provos. She had, further, disguised her voice with the simple device of a handkerchief over the receiver. ("Of course," Molly said when Nick told her, "she would never go any place without a handkerchief, hemstitched by hand.") She had ridden Ruth Bloom's bicycle to her father's funeral home and then driven the hearse to South Boston. After the crash she had cleaned the car and returned it to her father's garage. She knew it would not be used on Sunday. Funerals were never on Sunday, and she did the touch-up painting and put in new lenses while everyone was at Benediction on Sunday afternoon. Was she, on reflection, sorry? She was sorry about Agatha, but she was an innocent who had died in a state of grace. She was *very* sorry about the trooper—she had specified in the phone call that Mary Agnes come alone—and now she prayed he would make a full recovery. She regretted that she had to let Mrs. Bloom pay her for almost three extra hours. She was a sweet young woman, devoted to her husband.

"A furious mother, Molly," Nick said. "My psychology wasn't so bad. Used to doing everything herself. Able to cope. Had been doing plumbing and minor electric repairs for years, a lens was nothing. And Wendell Phillips? A long tongs, heavy, hotel quality, removed from the Athenaeum with the rest of the *batterie de cuisine* the next day."

"I still don't see how she expected to hit the right person, or confidently expected to hit anyone with the bust."

"I can only tell you what she says herself. She told Agatha to tell Mary Agnes to meet her in the reading room."

"Under the bust of Wendell Philips? How could any of them have given or taken instructions like that?"

"No, she only wanted to get her into the room; then she meant to call to her. I'm not sure she thought she could, assuredly, kill her. I think she just wanted to get at her, to frighten her. If she harmed her, well and good, but that wasn't essential. But then she killed Agatha, the little sister, whom she'd always mothered. And a few days later she learned that her son was dead, too. It was the second time, I think, that she really meant to get it right. She might well have gotten away with it, except that she could not let her sister, posthumously, ruin another innocent boy."

Molly told Nell that Mrs. Moran had confessed.

"Yes, she would," Nell said, "if suspicion focused on

someone else. I did see her and stop to talk with her in the gallery of the Athenaeum a few days before the party. She said she'd never been there before. It's so condescending to seem surprised if people show themselves curious about things that are new to them, I didn't press her about it. We hadn't heard, then, that the boy was dead; though I think his mother never expected to see him again after he left last winter. Then, that night at the Athenaeum after Agatha was killed, I felt sure she was responsible, because earlier when I'd looked for her to thank her I couldn't find her in the kitchen or anywhere else. I did go to Newnham to speak with her, Molly, but she cut me off entirely. I begged her to see a priest, not to go to the police, but to talk to someone for her own peace of mind, for her soul, I suppose. She denied everything. I knew she was lying and I blame myself. I did have guilty knowledge, Molly, and I let myself think I was shielding Mrs. Moran while all along I was hoping she would kill Mary Agnes."

"Nonetheless, you spoke with her, too," Molly said staunchly.

"I didn't *consciously* plan to cooperate in her murder. I went to see Mary Agnes the next day and told her that I believed someone was trying to kill her."

"And she didn't thank you for your troubles?"

"No, she said we couldn't intimidate her, neither stop her nor trick her into stopping. She said several unpleasant things about Alec, that he was using me to do his dirty work and wasn't manly himself and so forth."

"I've heard she was eloquent on that theme."

"She was hateful. But that policeman with her seemed such a rock, stolid and sensible. I thought I'd leave well enough alone, and then it began to dawn on me that I was the British consul's wife, so I left before anyone saw me. The Saturday night after Agatha's funeral, Anne Moran called me and said she was really frightened. A man had come Thursday night and left Patrick's medals, his religious medals—I don't know if they go in for posthumous decorations—and his diary, and now it was very late at night and she couldn't reach her mother. She had already called her aunt and was waiting for her to come. So I went out—first I called Mary Agnes to warn her. I didn't want to call her from the consulate, and Alec was away—but in any case, Mary Agnes had already left. I went to the Morans' and Sister Jude and I talked it over and she called Father Reynard. They were both afraid, I think, that Mary Magdalen might do something worse than she had done at Agatha's funeral, but they didn't know what it might be. I didn't tell them my suspicions—I couldn't bring myself to—but I did tell them I knew Mary Agnes was not at home either. They both leapt to the conclusion she was off somewhere with the Provos, and I thought Fergus McGonnigal might know what the IRA were up to, so I called him. He said he hadn't the least idea where they were meeting, but he'd be happy to help us look for Mrs. Moran and Senator O'Pake, either sister or both."

"And so you went looking for them," Molly asked, amazed, "all four of you?"

"We were going to search in pairs. I thought it would be a good idea to have one native, one foreigner in each car. I thought Sister Jude should drive with Fergus, and I'd go with the priest. We were about to leave when Kitty ran in and said the television show she was watching had just been interrupted to announce the accident. Bridget, Sister Jude that is, decided she should stay with the Moran girls, and the two men saw me home—they were both emphatic that I should not put my head out the door until Alec returned—and then they went to the scene, to administer last rites and to assist the police. Bridget called me as soon as her sister-in-law got home. She, of course, had been made to feel foolish—and I, because I was virtually certain about the other time, didn't know what to do."

"Nell, I didn't know what to think. Especially because you kept asking about Nick, despite your strictures about womanly reserve."

"Well, of course I asked you about him, child. I wanted to be sure you were getting to know him. You were made for each other. I saw it in a minute, didn't you?"

(20)

WINTHROP BOYDEN, returning without success from Moscow, took up to his room the packet of mail waiting for him at his London hotel. He opened first a small envelope from Molly, read through her note, crumpled it, opened it out again and, folding it smoothly, put it in the volume of Yeats by his bed, noting as he did words he had already underscored in "The Folly of Being Comforted," "not a crumb of comfort, not a grain." Then he turned to a longer letter from Hal Putnam, describing Mrs. Moran's indictment and suggesting he take over the defense. Liz had added a postscript, in her erratic hand that had been the despair of many nuns less wise than Sister Jude, begging him, as a favor to her, to come immediately. He began methodically to pack.

* * *

"Boyden is amazing, Molly," Nick said. "He's convinced Mrs. Moran to enter a plea of not guilty and, despite her confession, I think he may pull it off."

"He's very good," she agreed. "How's he defending her?"

"I think he's building a case for 'delayed heat of passion,' temporary insanity caused by brooding over grave injury. He's also hinting at some sort of preemptive self-defense. If Mary Agnes tried to involve the Moran girls in Eirelief, their mother might reasonably have feared she would lure them to a death like their brother's."

"Win's terrific. What he doesn't know about criminal procedure would fit on the head of a pin, along with everything you don't know about women." She sighed, utterly content. "And many, many angels."

"It's not just the technical things."

"It never is," she laughed.

"Thank you," he said, flattered. "But I was telling you about the trial. The D.A. doesn't always prosecute well, even when he's not ambivalent, as he plainly is about this case. And Boyden is remarkably astute. Father Reynard is there, ostensibly as Mrs. Moran's pastor, but I'm sure Boyden has taken his advice in selecting jurors: his peremptory challenges have been, no pun intended, inspired. And he's asked people questions he could not possibly have known to ask. Today he asked a roofer about possible justifications for killing tyrants and got a very thoughtful reply."

"I haven't seen Win since he got back; but I wrote to him."

"I thought you must have. We met for the first time today and he congratulated me. He's impressive. Stoic."

*   *   *

Dr. Brewster, with the results of a privately conducted poll in his breast pocket—he hoped he would not have to show it to Bess: it indicated that against five randomly selected names (they had done it three ways, all Italian and all Irish and mixed) she could not hope for more than seven percent of the vote—came cheerfully to lunch. "Scotty's office has been trying most urgently to reach you, dear. They wouldn't tell me what it was about. I expect it's a very great tribute to you."

It was a high point, truly a red-letter day in the evolution of the two-career marriage, Christopher Boggle said at the farewell party he and a transmogrified Mrs. Boggle (the threatening calls were never traced to her) gave the Brewsters before they left for Geneva. He congratulated Molly that day, too. "I was so happy to hear of your latest engagement, Ms. Rafferty. It's so much better for you professionally. If this marriage comes to pass, the Vatican Archives, at least, will remain open to you."

The chairman of the Physics Department, Clara Meicklejohn, overheard his felicitations and swore (as she now did hourly) that while she breathed he would not be president of Scattergood. She had vigorously assented earlier when a radical anthropologist said she longed for a day when women could kill for their ideals and institutions, not just their offspring, and be acquitted.

Molly replied mildly that she hoped they would always be as happy as the Boggles themselves, but that she must find Nick, who had gone into the garden with Dr. Brewster, because they needed to get to Woods Hole by nine to catch the last ferry for Martha's Vineyard.

"I wonder if the trains, I mean the ferries, will be running on time," Boggle said. "I am sure your fiancé, devoted as he must be to law and order, will prefer that they do."

It was then that Miss Meicklejohn threw the potted shrimp at Boggle and the sentiment for her crystallized. Clara Meicklejohn became, that fall, the eleventh president of Scattergood.

Molly protested to Cornelia Newman, Clerk of the Faculty Meeting, that although academic freedom might be stretched to protect utterances such as Boggle's and they might not be justified in stripping him of tenure, he had shown himself unfit to be dean. She would resign from the college if he remained in his post. Mrs. Newman said she had already proposed he be suspended, but it was up to Clara. Molly must know that there were people indebted to Boggle. He had countenanced questionable hirings and presided over some appalling terminations. All in all, he had served as *padrone* for those of the faculty without scholarly reputations. It had been very bad for Scattergood that Bess had left him so free a hand with junior appointments. Clara Meicklejohn herself called Molly a few days later and said, "You've heard we're losing Boggle? Would you like to be dean when you get back from Florence?"

"I'm honored, truly, to be asked," she said. "But I want to have a baby next year. I expect to teach and write while our children are little, but I don't think I could manage the deanship."

"I think that's very sensible," Miss Meicklejohn assured her. "I wish you joy."

Christopher Boggle left Scattergood a few weeks later

to assume the presidency of a small, lavishly endowed evangelical college in Texas. The school's chief benefactor had demanded it be offered to him. His own daughter had gone to an elite eastern college and been taught nothing but race mixing and collectivism by some mackerel-snapping Red. Boggle was the only Christian he had met in that Gehenna.

Gerald Harrigan emerged victorious from a fratricidal Democratic primary and the Holy Sepulchre Alumnae arranged a debate between him and the Republican challenger, a political newcomer, Henry Hughes Putnam, who had handily defeated his primary opponent, a libertarian podiatrist accused of Medicare fraud. It promised to be a media event. In the debate, which was to be televised, the two men would first address each other and then take questions from the floor; the candidates' families were to be interviewed beforehand. Daniel Bloom, moving increasingly out of his academic specialty and into political commentary and cultural criticism, had agreed to ruminate, at its conclusion, upon what it all signified.

Molly thought she would prefer to watch it alone. "It's ridiculous, I know, but I feel awkward about being with you while we watch each other watching him," she told Nick.

"I won't insist, but I'd like to stay. Would you feel better about it if I told you that when I was twenty years old I made love to Kathleen Harrigan, Kathleen Mulcahy she was then, in the blackest desperation?"

"Harrigan's wife, Mulcahy's daughter, *she's* Kathleen?"

"Yes. I was at my wit's end. I thought I could make her love me. She went to bed with me willingly enough, but marriage was out of the question."

"Oh, darling, no wonder the Harrigans depressed you. She must be a most unfeeling woman." She switched on the set. "She looks flawless and *very* determined."

"She adds a certain tone to his campaign. Real candid brow, don't you think? Wait till you hear her."

Kathleen Harrigan was saying that nothing on earth mattered more to her husband—that was why he was so committed to what good people everywhere were feeling about the family—than their own family, their home, their children, their—she looked full into the camera and then lowered her eyes—their marriage. "I could not begin to count the ways I love my husband, as the poetess says."

"Nick, I can't believe it."

"I've nothing to say except to recall to you the view that betrothals are binding."

"Wait," Molly said. "You've met Dan but you haven't heard him on the *Zeitgeist* yet."

Liz Putnam did not discuss conjugal matters. She spoke in more general terms about the value of competition. All voters, she thought, were better served by having every seat vigorously contested. She hoped they would listen to the debate, ask any questions that occurred to them, and thereafter vote as they saw fit. Her grandfather, John Hennessy, who in 1928 had overcome prejudice to become the district's first Democratic congressman, had never run unopposed and he had never forgotten what he owed his constituents.

Harrigan, after some soul-searching and extensive polling, had decided to run to the right of Putnam. Hal Putnam was known to have brought Winthrop Boyden back from Europe to defend the woman who had confessed to murdering Harrigan's strongest rival in the primary, possibly the strongest Democratic candidate in the general election. There was much sympathy for Mrs. Moran, too. No one really knew how the chips would fall on that. But Harrigan came out swinging on law and order. What had been Putnam's role in this travesty of justice, the acquittal of Mary Magdalen Moran?

Hal Putnam upheld the rule of law. No sane person would wish crime to be committed with impunity. Mrs. Moran had been arrested, indicted, and tried. She had been acquitted, not on technicalities, but by a jury of her peers who had flatly refused to convict her. The community must defend itself against violence, but it was the common sense of the community, expressed by the twelve men and women of the jury, that had unanimously held her innocent. Certainly his good friend Winthrop Boyden had stated the case clearly. He, for one, was grateful to him for doing it so well. But a group of citizens, like the voters, like the people here tonight, had made the decision.

Then Harrigan made his mistake. "Mr. Putnam," he said, "you are countenancing the law of the jungle, you are licensing the *vendetta*."

"*Vendetta?*" Putnam repeated the word slowly and musically. "No, I don't think so. The practice of the vendetta, although you use the Italian word for it, Mr. Harrigan, is an almost universal, and I think a perfectly natural, response to the inability of civil authorities to secure order. It occurs everywhere before nation-states are securely established. It is not the case here. Mrs. Moran was apprehended by officers of the Commonwealth and tried according to our criminal law. I have every confidence in our police, though I wish there were more of them and they were better paid."

"Not bad," said Nick.

"Not bad at all," Molly replied. "He must have done more than row at Harvard. I wonder whether he did history or sociology."

Liz Putnam asked her husband the same thing later. "Hal, how did you think up that bit about the vendetta?"

"Common sense," he replied.

Harrigan was on the ropes after that. Someone asked him about terrorism. He deplored it but thought, *in extremis*, people might resort to it. Putnam said nothing about the IRA, but made several pointed criticisms of the PLO, thus nailing down three wards in Harrigan's own town, where some felt that Tatiana Alexievna had been left in the lurch and voter turnout was reliably high.

When questions were invited from the audience, Sister Jude said nothing about abortion but pressed Harrigan on Central America. He got the chronology wrong in one place and muddled the regimes in another. Liz Putnam had assured Margaret Donahue that, although she revered Sister Jude and contributed to Holy Sepulchre herself, she had threatened to leave Hal if he advocated public subsidies for parochial schools. Margaret did not, therefore, mention tuition tax credits but asked instead about welfare reform, permitting Putnam to discuss family allowances in some detail.

"It was a well-run debate," Hal's mother said. "I don't

see why you won't join the Holy Sepulchre Alumnae, Liz. They are just like the League of Women Voters, perhaps a little brighter."

"Perhaps you are right, Julia." Liz's mother-in-law rarely made suggestions, but Liz had found that when she did it was well to follow them.

"Putnam was the clear winner," Daniel Bloom announced, "but given the registration in the district, Harrigan looks certain to be elected."

"Yes, and we shall want to hear more of your analysis, Professor Bloom, but first, tell us something about yourself," the anchorwoman from Channel 9 said, crossing her remarkable legs. "How do you manage, in this age of specialization, to remain a Renaissance man?"

"There is such a thing as blasphemy," Nick said. But Molly was helpless with laughter, and neither of them heard much about his early life and researches. They were quieter when he got to his second marriage and the power of erotic love to impart metaphysical insights.

"Where is he getting this?" Nick asked. "Did you tell him about Catherine of Siena?"

"No, I didn't. It's cabalistic or Hasidic. Universal, darling, like the vendetta. Every tradition has mystics and ecstatic convulsives."

"And glorious some of them are. But he seems to be putting all that to base purposes here."

The anchorwoman did seem enchanted. She hoped he would tell her audience more about that fascinating subject very soon. He said he'd be delighted any time and returned to civic virtue.

"Oh, God," Molly said, "here comes socialism and the loss of élan vital."

"Neither candidate advocated socialism or lacked élan vital."

"It's just in passing," Molly explained.

"Yes, I see. He's winding up with authenticity and ethnicity and plunking for Harrigan."

The young woman from Channel 9 had drawn Bloom out marvelously. She felt it a milestone in her career; and Bloom had never been better, except that he called it wrong. Hal Putnam became in November the first Republican elected from the district since 1926. They said, in the bars in Hooley Square, it couldn't have happened if the Church hadn't had a hand in it.